I0563407

RACHEL SINCLAIR

JUSTICE DELAYED

VINCI

BOOKS

By Rachel Sinclair

Southern California Legal Thrillers

Presumed Guilty

Justice Delayed

Insanity Defense

Wrongful Conviction

The Trial

Vinci Books

vinci-books.com

Published by Vinci Books Ltd in 2025

1

Copyright © Rachel Sinclair 2019

The author has asserted their moral right to be identified as the author of this work in accordance with the Copyright, Designs and Patents Act 1988. This work is a work of fiction. Names, characters, places and incidents are the product of the author's imagination or are used fictitiously. Any resemblance to actual persons, living or dead, places and incidents is entirely coincidental.

All rights reserved. No part of this publication may be copied, reproduced, distributed, stored in any retrieval system, or transmitted in any form or by any means, including photocopying, recording, or other electronic or mechanical methods, nor used as a source for any form of machine learning including AI datasets, without the prior written permission of the publisher.

The publisher and the author have made every effort to obtain permissions for any third party material used in this book and to comply with copyright law. Any queries in this respect should be brought to the attention of the publisher and any omissions will be corrected in future editions.

A CIP catalogue record for this book is available from the British Library.

Paperback ISBN: 9781036702915

Chapter One

AVERY

Present Day

I COULDN'T BELIEVE what I was hearing. Apparently, Regina had managed to track down at least some of the people responsible for putting me in prison all those years ago. Could it be true? After having spent seven years of my life on a hard cot, eating crappy food, and feeling in my heart all those years a sense of burning injustice, I would have my chance to maybe, just maybe, see that justice was done. As I spent all those years in prison, all that I could think about, day after day, was getting back at the people who did this to me.

Regina and I had made a date to meet at a restaurant in Imperial Beach, which was where Regina's condo was. SEA180 was an upscale beachfront restaurant with an enormous deck and fire pits all around. It was a cool evening, as September evenings sometimes were, especially close to the ocean. The temperature around the water tended to be about 10° cooler than the mainland as it was, and around October or November, the weather cooled off considerably. Especially at night. I remembered watching the girls in the movie *LaLa Land*, when they were going to the producer's party in little tiny dresses in the middle of December and thinking about how unrealistic that was. While the temperatures never got to a freezing point, as in other parts of the country during the wintertime, it certainly wasn't tiny dress weather.

But September tended to be a little bit warmer than it was tonight. Nevertheless, I found a seat on the deck. I made sure we had a fire pit in front of us, and I closed my eyes and listened to the water coming in. I had to calm myself a bit. What Regina was about to tell me would change my life. And, once she told me, what would I say? How would I approach it? I wanted to take everybody down, one by one. I wanted to burn each one of them at the stake. But I would have to go through this methodically. I certainly could not just pell-mell, willy-nilly stab each person in the back.

Regina met me at 8 o'clock. It was a little late for dinner, but she couldn't meet until that time. I passed the time waiting for her by sipping on a dirty martini made with Grey Goose vodka, my go-to cocktail when I was feeling out of sorts. My stomach was doing flip-flops.

She sat down across from me. "You want to get an appetizer?" she asked me. "I'm really in the mood for some raw oysters, for some reason."

I motioned to the seat right across from mine. "Oysters are fine," I said to her. "Now tell me what you found out."

Her green eyes were dancing. "Well, here's what I found. Do you know about the case of Jeffrey Epstein?" she asked.

I nodded. And when she said that name, I immediately flashed back to that day in the pool with Becky. The memory was vague, and it was something buried some-where in my psyche. But I remembered her talking to me about a middle-aged man who was interested in her. In fact, she told me she had sex with this middle-aged man. "Yes. I do know the name of Jeffrey Epstein."

"So you know what that bastard was accused of doing, right? I mean, he's dead now, of course, but in life, do you know what he did? He was a sex trafficker. He got these young girls to service his wealthy and powerful friends." Regina shook her head, a disgusted look on her face. "It's disgusting. What that dude was doing, there should be the death penalty for that one. And you know how I feel about the death penalty."

I was surprised to hear Regina talking about the death penalty in that way. But I could see she was serious. She generally was very much against the state putting people to death because she'd witnessed an execution. Her father was shot and killed by a guy high on PCP. She saw her father's killer die by lethal injection. She told me she was against the death penalty after that point in time.

"I do know how you feel about the death penalty, and I'm surprised to hear you say something like that. What made you change your mind?"

She shook her head. "I'm just blowing off steam. But what he was doing was absolutely disgusting. Do you know Jeffrey Epstein was friends with both Bill Clinton and Donald Trump? And Prince Andrew. All of them are known dogs. So yeah, these guys were getting their freak on with young vulnerable girls."

I thought about what Regina was saying and I wondered if Becky was involved in something like that. I definitely wouldn't have been surprised if she was after what she told me by the pool that one day. "Are you saying Becky was involved in a ring like that?"

"That's what I'm saying. There's a house in Del Mar, high on a cliff, belongs to a dude named Carl Williams."

My heart started to race. I remembered Becky had talked to me about an older guy by the name of Carl. I also remembered she talked about visiting him out here in San Diego. She told me he had big parties out here and she was hoping to meet men through him who would help her break into the movie industry.

At the time, I thought it was odd that her parents allowed her to visit him out here from her home in Kansas City. But her parents were extremely permissive. Too permissive. And she did fly out and visit him just about every weekend.

What was she doing during those weekends?

"Carl Williams. Who is he? What does he do?"

"Near as I can tell, the guy don't do shit. I mean, he does, but he makes his money off other people. It's not like he's actually contributing to the country. He manages some hedge fund for a lot of other billionaires. He doesn't create anything, he doesn't employ anybody, all he does is manage a lot of investments. And, apparently, he makes quite a lot of money off his sex trafficking ring as well. He gets a lot of money from his rich friends to kiddy diddle these young girls. And, when I say young girls, I mean young girls. We're talking 14 years old, and the oldest girls apparently are 17. I have no idea why these rich fucks like to get with these young girls, but apparently they do."

I took a sip of my dirty martini as I thought about what she was telling me. This Carl guy, he must've had Becky as part of his stable of girls. I wondered if Carl himself was the person responsible for Becky dying. If he was, what could I do? I would have to get some kind of evidence against him, but that seemed impossible at this point. Becky was murdered 20 years ago. I knew there was DNA evidence and evidence that she was raped, but the DNA was never matched up with anybody. That was the problem with DNA evidence – it only works to incriminate somebody if their DNA was already on file somewhere. In this case, apparently the person who had raped Becky had not been arrested before raping her, so his DNA wasn't on file. If he had been arrested before raping her, we probably would've already had him nailed to the wall.

"And what are you going to do? Also, how did you find out about this Carl Williams guy and what he was doing?"

She smiled. "I still know my girls. The girls from the street. I'm still in touch with all of them, at least the ones who are still alive."

She looked sad when she said that last line. I knew Regina had lost quite a few friends along the way. That was the perils of the street - you don't always last very long.

"And who told you about Carl and what he was doing?"

"There's this girl, name's Jean. I don't know if that's her real name, but that's the name that she goes by. Jean. She's one of the lucky ones who got out of the game. She's working as a dental assistant. It's kind of embarrassing for her, as some of her old johns come into see her dentist from time to time, and they both kind of pretend they don't know each other. Anyhow, I've been talking to the girls on the street. I've been taking your friend's picture around to them, asking them if they know her. Listen, when you told me a rich bastard was possibly behind Becky's murder, the first thing I thought about was sex trafficking. I've known far too many rich guys who get into all kinds of kinky stuff and far too many rich guys who get into young girls. So I knew that if I talked to all the girls I know in the business or were in the business, I could figure it out. And, well, Jean knows Becky. Or she knew her."

I nodded. "How old is Jean?"

Regina shrugged her shoulders. "I don't know, but I would guess she's probably around our age. Around 35. It's kinda hard to know how old she is, but that's how old she looks. She's had a hard life, so she's a little bit beat up, but she's had work done, so she's not so bad off. Anyhow, I talked to her. She knew Becky. She told me she knew Becky through the sex ring she used to work. She told me about the parties this Carl Williams would have, she told me about the girls they used, everything. I asked her if she would ever go to the police and tell them what she knew, but she told me she would never do that."

"Why not?" I knew the answer to that, but I wondered what Jean told Regina.

"She said she was scared, but I think it was something more than that. I think she told me that Carl and all of his friends had what they call immunity from prosecution. In other words, they all think they're above the law, and maybe they are. Jean said they own the prosecutor's office and own the cops as well. Apparently, Carl has all of the prosecutor's office and the cops on his payroll."

Again, I knew what Regina was talking about. Those rich fucks do tend to be above the law because they owned too many people in law enforcement.

"Go on," I said.

Regina nodded. "Jean told me that Carl has a long list of people he can blackmail to ensure he stays out of trouble. He hides video cameras all over his place. And every time a guy comes into the place and finds a girl and bangs her, it's all captured on video. And we're talking thousands of guys over the years. All of these guys have relatives who care about them. For whatever reason. And some of the guys who partake in the festivities are prosecutors themselves. And cops. So because of this practice of videotaping everybody, he's got the goods on a lot of people in the prosecutor's office and in the police force. So, in other words, if he can't bribe them, he blackmails them. So Jean told me it was pointless to go to the cops to ask to press charges against Carl and his friends because she knew nothing would ever come of it."

"I mean, think about it," Regina continued. "This house in Del Mar has been the site of all these shenanigans for all these years, and nobody has ever heard about it. Why do you think that is? Why do you think the cops haven't busted in the door by now? It seems like this guy Carl is airtight. As Jean said, he's immune from prosecution. And not in a good way."

The waiter came around and brought Regina and me some chilled oysters on a silver platter. I took one, swallowed it with some cocktail sauce, and then took a sip of my dirty martini. "Immune from prosecution. Immune from prosecution." The term "immunity from prosecution" usually meant the person literally had some kind of recognized immunity. Like, for instance, ambassadors from other countries had diplomatic immunity. That meant they could commit a crime while on American soil, but if they committed the crime while in their role of a diplomat, they were not to be prosecuted. But most people weren't above the law.

Most people weren't. However, I knew the world we lived in, and I knew that you could get out of anything if you had enough money. Apparently, this Carl Williams also knew this.

"Do you think Carl was behind Becky's murder?"

Regina sat back in her chair and took a bite of her olive. She, like me, enjoyed her dirty martinis. "I haven't gotten that far. However, I think I'm on the right track. After all, that kid, that Brad Whitmore kid, told you the person responsible for her murder was extremely wealthy. Carl fits the bill and he was involved with Becky. He's also involved in a sex trafficking ring. He's looking pretty good for Becky's murder. Then again, I have no proof of anything. I don't even have proof he has a sex trafficking ring going on. I'm going to have to do a little bit of homework on this entire matter."

"What kind of homework?"

"Undercover work. It's something I haven't done before, but something I'd like to do. Listen, you have to remember one thing – I was a sex worker. I know the lines, I know the moves, and I know the johns. I know their psychology better than any shrink. I could possibly go to this Carl guy and hit him up for a job. I don't think he'd actually hire me to be one of the girls in his stable. Because, like I said before, they like very young girls in this ring. I'm obviously not a very young girl. But Jean told me this Carl guy was always looking for an older girl to be a mother figure for the younger ones. Carl apparently has about 10 live-in girls. He still might. Mainly, the girls don't live there with him – some of the girls he got from rich people would still be living with their parents, but they'd visit Carl and his buddies while telling their parents they're going out for the night with their girlfriends or whatever."

"So most of the girls were day players, so to speak. But he has girls who live there with him too?"

She nodded. "Yes. We're talking about the runaways. He finds girls off the streets, or, rather, he'd recruit them off the streets. And that's where I come in. Maybe. My plan is to go to this Carl person and try to find a job with him. He can hire me to maybe recruit the girls or to be the house mother, or maybe even to do both. Jean told me he has women doing both jobs a lot of the time. If I can convince Carl I'm his girl, his house mother, I'm in. Once I'm in, I know exactly how to do my investigation. I know how to talk to the girls and I know how to cover my tracks. Not only that, I can figure out what the vulnerabilities are in his security system. If I could possibly get Christian to hack into this dude's files, we're golden."

I thought about what she was saying. It made a lot of sense. And I knew she'd do a good job. I also knew one other thing – Regina was drop-dead gorgeous. Olive skin, dark hair, light green eyes that were so bright they could probably be seen in the dark. Her body was perfect – gorgeous breasts, slim waist, tight legs and butt. She wasn't anybody who would flaunt her gorgeousness. She pretty much dressed down in jeans and T-shirts, her thick dark hair usually up in a ponytail, her face usually unadorned of makeup. But I knew that if she really put her mind to it that she could easily make herself beautiful enough that this Carl person would hire her in a flash. Especially if she told him about her background and how she knew how to recruit people, how she knew how to find a vulnerable girl, and how she knew how to take care of young girls. Regina told me this was something she had some experience with, as her boyfriend/pimp, Michael, often had her do this for him. He had her go to bus stations and airports, but especially bus stations, to look for girls who looked lost and frightened and possibly were runaways. That was one thing she felt shamed about – finding young women for Michael's stable.

I wondered if it could work. And even if it could work, who was to say Regina could find enough proof to show Carl was behind Becky's murder? It made sense that he was behind it somehow because he had the power and influence to make sure everybody involved in this case would dance to his tune. But how would we ever prove it? That was the thing.

I chewed on my bottom lip as I thought about my dilemma. Regina was telling me something a part of me already knew. I wanted her to go with her plan. I would try very hard to find some kind of proof this Carl was behind murdering Becky. But if I couldn't, maybe there would be some other way to bring him down.

In fact, I knew there would be a way to bring him down. The prosecutor's office was completely dirty, so there would be no way in hell they would ever move against this guy. The cops were also dirty, so they, too, refused to do anything against him. Even if all that was true, I could still bring this bastard to justice. It might not be perfect justice. Perfect justice, in this case, would mean Carl would end up in an orange jumpsuit for the rest of his life, and, as a sex offender, specifically a child rapist, he would definitely experience the worst kind of treatment in prison. But I knew this might not happen.

However, even if it didn't happen, there was another way I could bring him down. It involved the legal system, and it involved Regina doing her job well enough to convince at least a few of the girls to turn against Carl. If she could do that, we would be on our way. I wouldn't even need the cooperation of the prosecutors, the cops, or anybody else.

"When are you going to see this Carl, and how are you going to approach him? I mean, I'm assuming this Jean person, since she's now working in a dentist's office, probably doesn't have a line to Carl anymore. I assume Carl's activities are underground, to say the very least. He can't just trust anybody off the street. I mean, what you gonna do, just go to his house, knock on the door, and ask him for a job? That'll never work."

"Of course, that won't work. Listen, I have contacts everywhere. Not just on the street, but I have other contacts that will help me out in this situation. I've got people who can vouch for me to Carl. I'm just going to have to hit up my contacts and call in a few favors. There are quite a few people who owe me a favor. It's just a matter of finding the right person who knows Carl and has his ear."

"And who are you thinking about?"

She nodded. "Listen, I've been doing my homework on this Carl person. And I do know one thing – he doesn't just hang out with other rich dudes like him. I mean, he hangs out with other rich dudes, but some of those rich dudes who hang out with him aren't exactly managing hedge funds themselves. Some of the guys who hang out there are CEOs, politicians, athletes and actors. People with a respectable job by day, and by night, want to get their freak on with a very young girl. But I also found out that some of the rich dudes who hang out with Carl are guys in the industry, just like Carl, but not quite as savory. If you know what I mean."

I knew exactly what Regina meant. Organized crime. "Who are you talking about? Russians, Albanians, Armenians, Mexicans?" I knew the Italian Mafia wasn't very strong in Southern California. In fact, the Italian Mafia wasn't that strong west of Las Vegas. But in Southern California, other ethnic groups certainly ran rampant.

"I know a guy by the name of Sergei Popov. And I've

talked to him. He's a friend of mine. I asked him about Carl's ring and he told me he wants to meet with me tomorrow night. It sounds like he knows something about it, probably knows people involved in it. I don't know, but I'm hoping he can lead me to somebody who can get me into Carl's inner circle."

When she was talking, I started feeling a sense of hope. I felt like there was a chance to finally get some closure on everything that happened and finally get a measure of justice. It was just a matter of Regina finding out what she needed to find out and then hopefully put the pieces together.

"Listen, Regina, you be careful." While Regina was street-wise, I didn't know if she was used to infiltrating such a high-level world as what she was volunteering to do for me. I knew that people, when they go undercover, were taking their lives into their own hands. If anything happened to Regina because she was working for me, I could never forgive myself.

"Trust me, I got this. I've worked with much more dangerous people than Sergei Popov and his entire creepy clan. I'll be careful, but really, it's not necessary to say that."

I had a wrap in my purse, and I brought it out and wrapped it around my shoulders. I put my feet up on the edge of the fire ring and leaned back. It was a perfect evening for a glass of wine and relaxation. My big trial was over, Esme Gutierrez was a free woman, and there was the possibility that Regina could bring this whole thing home.

At that moment, life was good.

Tomorrow, it might be a different story. But for tonight, I was content to just listen to the sounds of the ocean rolling in and out while I sat on the patio of a luxury restaurant.

Chapter Two

REGINA

REGINA KNEW what she had to do. It wasn't anything that she looked forward to, yet she knew that if wanted into the inner circle of Carl Williams, she would have to go back to her sex worker days. She had the muscle memory for it. It would be just like riding a bike. Yet she didn't want to sell her body. And she certainly didn't want to do what she would have to, which was to go out on the streets and find young girls. Her plan was to help Avery with what the two of them had talked about at the restaurant the night before – Regina was to find these girls and use them to testify against Carl in a court of law.

Regina needed to help Avery find victims in Carl's circle, talk to them in a way only she could, and see what they could do as far as suing Carl. Avery would also do what she could about going to the prosecutor's office and the police and see if they'd be interested in prosecuting these people. But Regina and Avery both held out little hope that such a move would go anywhere. Carl was just too powerful and he had too many people in his pocket for the two of them to have any hope these people would do the right thing. So it was up to Avery to financially bring this entire thing down.

It wouldn't be just the fact that these girls would be suing this bastard, but also the media attention surrounding such a sensational lawsuit would be devastating to Carl. It was all a matter of finding enough girls willing to go against him. And also to be mindful of the statute of limitations, which was two years for sexual misconduct. The advantage in this case, however, was that the victims were minors. They would almost all be under the age of 18, which meant the statute of limitations didn't start running for them.

At the same time, Regina wasn't sure that Carl was behind Becky's murder. She only knew that he was behind exploiting her. And she had a good feeling that, no matter what, the fact that Becky was being exploited was, in the end, the cause of her being killed. She also had a strong feeling that Carl had to have been behind the murder in some way because he would've been powerful enough to have corrupted the prosecutor. She'd already gone through the records on what happened with Becky's case, and she knew exactly why her friend was convicted for her murder.

The prosecutor in that case was a guy by the name of Paul Sharpton. She already had Christian hack his bank records for the period of time when he was apparently on the take from Carl. Christian couldn't find any kind of large transfer from Carl to Paul. Christian combed through all the bank transactions and came up empty.

Regina had to figure that one out too. Why was Paul so willing to make sure that Avery was convicted for the murder of Becky if he wasn't being bribed to do so? Regina figured it was something else. She knew that when corruption happened, it usually happened for one of two reasons.

Either the corrupted person was being bribed or being blackmailed. In her experience, the second scenario was much more powerful. The first scenario was powerful for greedy people. But to be greedy enough to send an innocent girl to prison for the rest of her life, that took a special kind of sociopath. Only a person without a conscience could do such a thing for money.

But, if it was a blackmail situation, all bets were off. People had a survival instinct. If they were presented with the choice between their life, or exposure of something they did, or exposure of something that someone they loved did, and the life of another, they were going to choose self-preservation every time.

Every time.

So that was something Regina would have to figure out. Exactly why Paul Sharpton did what he did. And if she could figure that out, what his big secret was, she could expose him. And if she could expose him, that would be another way Avery could get some justice on what happened to her. Because, in the end, although Regina could understand the need to self preserve, that didn't excuse what he did. Nothing could ever excuse him withholding crucial evidence from the court in the case.

There was something else unusual about Paul Sharpton. After Avery's murder case, he moved from Kansas City to San Diego. He'd been in the San Diego County prosecutor's office for the past 20 years or so. Other than the fact that his presence in the prosecutor's office made Avery sick every time he was on the other side of one of her case's, Regina wondered if Paul's move was significant in some way.

Regina also suspected that Gloria Flores, Avery's public defender, was dirty. She'd reviewed the file carefully and if

Gloria wasn't dirty, she was spectacularly incompetent. One or the other. She suspected corruption on Gloria's part as well, however.

She would do what she could to make sure everybody went down for Avery's imprisonment. Starting with Carl.

She made a date with Sergei for that night. Sergei was a very attractive Russian man, a Boyevik in a Russian clan by the name of Ivanov. The Ivanov clan ruled Southern California. They were into trafficking, drug dealing, extortion, gun running and illegal gambling. As a Boyevik, which was the equivalent of a soldier in the Italian Mafia, Sergei was responsible for trafficking women for the Ivanov clan. He wasn't involved in Carl's circle, however, as Carl strictly dealt with underaged girls and Sergei was only into trafficking women who weren't underaged. He concentrated on women between the ages of 21 and 25, recruiting them for an underground high-class nightclub in a nondescript building by the Embarcadero, right across from where the cruise ships docked on the waterfront. Regina had visited this club, mainly because she was curious, and before she got a job as a private investigator for Avery, she thought she might end up working at just such a club.

The reason why this club was underground and not an out and proud strip club, such as the clubs that dotted boulevards all over the San Diego area, from Point Loma to Miramar, was that it was a front for a prostitution ring. Strip clubs generally had neon signs that advertised the wares within. Some of the clubs featured fully nude dancers and their websites advertised exactly that.

But the club the Ivanov family ran was a different beast altogether. This was a very exclusive club, as members paid $1000 and up per month to belong. And the reason for this was simple – the girls were providing not just a show for the gentlemen who frequented the club, but the girls on display could also be bought. The club featured a number of various rooms where men could indulge their every fantasy. For instance, for men who were into bondage and discipline, there was a room outfitted with an enormous St. Andrew's cross as well as a whipping post, chains, leather suits, anything a well-heeled gentleman would desire. There was an orgy room which was just as it sounded – it was a room where groups of people would get together and have sex. There were a variety of other rooms that attracted men just looking to have a good time but were into a more vanilla variety of a sexual experience.

The girls would dance for the men in the main part of the building, most of them completely nude, and if a man desired a more intimate encounter with any one woman, he was entitled to that. With his membership, he was entitled to one free encounter every month. After that, he had to pay by the hour. The fees ranged from $500 per hour for a vanilla encounter, all the way up to $2000 per hour for an encounter that involved humiliating and degrading the woman he chose. The girls got a certain percentage of the fees these men paid, generally 30%, and the house kept the rest.

Regina's feminist instincts were appalled by such an arrangement. As far as she was concerned, if a girl agreed to be humiliated, which sometimes involved literally getting pissed or defecated on, she was certainly entitled to more than $600 per hour, which was what she got from the house while the Ivanovs took the rest of the $2000 per hour. For something like that, Regina would certainly demand more than $600 per hour.

But she wouldn't lecture anybody about their business practices. It wasn't her affair.

Sergei found the women who worked in this particular club. The women who worked in the club ranged from women who were bored housewives who worked the day shift while the kids were in school to professionals who had been in the business for years to college students working on their master's degrees. Because every woman in this club was older than 21, Sergei didn't try to recruit undergrads unless they were in their senior year.

It was important that the girls were 21 and clean because this was the understanding the police had about this club. Regina knew that Yuri Ivanov, the Pakhan of the Ivanov clan, which meant he was the head of it, had an arrangement with the police force in the San Diego area. For this particular club, the cops got 20% of the club's gross in exchange for not raiding the place. But the private agreement between Yuri and the police force was that the girls had to be at least 21. The reason for that was pretty simple, really. Girls older than 21 knew what they were getting into and weren't being exploited.

On the other hand, if the girls were not of age, that would be a problem. Younger girls were ripe for being exploited. Regina knew that in order to find younger girls, they couldn't fish from the same pool as the Ivanov club did. They couldn't find the bored housewives, the girls working on their PhDs, the long time professionals, the models trying to make it. No. With the younger girls, the trafficking generally involved either kidnapping, nabbing runaways, or, as in Regina's case, finding girls with difficult home lives who were looking to get out.

In other words, when you go younger, it necessarily involved exploitation. And that, apparently, was a bridge too far for the police force. They didn't agree to lay off of the Ivanov club if any of the girls were under the age of 21.

Therefore, Sergei was very careful about checking their IDs and if anybody didn't check out, she wasn't offered a position there.

Regina, in a way, didn't mind what Sergei did for the Ivanov clan. She was of the mindset that when you are free, white, and 21 - so to speak, as the girls who worked these clubs were from every walk of life and every ethnic background - the girls were free to do as they pleased. They were paid well for what they did, they walked into the club with their eyes opened, nobody was forcing them, and they generally were not vulnerable to exploitation.

Sergei arrived at the restaurant. The Gaslamp Strip Club, where they agreed to meet, was a steakhouse in the Gaslamp District of San Diego. The restaurant was a perfect blend of old and new. The walls were composed of exposed brick and the ceilings were a good 30 feet high. Black leather circular booths surrounding red tables lined up along a glass wall, giving the place a retro feel, while the tables in the middle of the hard-wood floor restaurant were composed of light wood with white chairs that sported rectangular backs with a hole cut in the middle of them. The bar was a typical bar, but the chandeliers were in the shape of enormous snowflakes. The chandeliers looked almost like a mobile, with uneven spokes coming out in the middle of the chandelier, and each spoke had a small light on the end of it. The menu at this place was that of a typical steakhouse and the prices ranged from $18 for a skirt steak to $30 for a 20 ounce porterhouse steak. All sides were extra, three for $19.

This place was a tad fancy for Regina. She was a burger and fries girl - In 'n' Out was her favorite restaurant. When she couldn't get into In 'n' Out, which was often the case, as their lines were hellacious, her second favorite place was

Five Guys Burger and Fries, and when she was feeling particularly fancy, she might go to the Burger Lounge in the Hillcrest area. The fries with the ranch dressing there were to die for.

But this place - she had to dress up a little. That was one thing she didn't like to do. Just as she preferred burgers and fries to overpriced steaks, she preferred jeans and T-shirts to dresses and heels. But she also knew that Sergei, even though he was nothing but a soldier in his organization, was a classy guy. He was the kind of guy who liked dark jazz clubs instead of loud nightclubs, telling Regina that she hadn't lived until she saw Esperanza Spalding or Gregory Porter performing live. He liked his martinis dry and neat, his steaks medium rare, and his women in tiny black dresses with cleavage.

She shifted in her seat and looked around. As usual, she saw admiring glances from men around the room. Not that she cared about that because she didn't. Men weren't on her agenda and never were. After all, she'd never had a good encounter with one. From her mother's boyfriends who hit on her, one of whom raped her, to Michael, who beat and exploited her, her experiences with men hadn't been positive.

Men were people she could utilize and that was that.

Sergei finally arrived at the restaurant. Sergei was tall and fit, about 6'3", with sandy blonde hair and big blue eyes. His face was angular with a strong jaw line and a perfect Roman nose. With his bow-shaped lips and light blue eyes, he almost resembled a young Paul Newman, albeit much taller than Paul Newman. With his enormous dimples and thousand watt smile, Sergei was quite the head turner himself. If Regina was inclined to date anybody, she would probably date a guy like Sergei. Yes he was involved in some unsavory business with the Ivanov club. Yet he wasn't a sex trafficker, per se, but, rather, he was a guy who knew how to talk women into working for this club. Of all the jobs he could've done for the Ivanov family, his was the least objectionable.

He saw her and made a beeline for the table she was sitting. She stood up and gave Sergei a purposeful and sincere hug. "Sergei, dude, what's going on?" she asked him as he hugged her.

He laughed at her calling him "dude." "Well, chick, I was wondering the same thing. When you called me, I got very excited." He nodded as he looked Regina over. "You know, Regina, the girls at my club age out at the age of 25. But I could certainly make an exception for you. You've kept yourself up beautifully."As he said that, he was staring at her legs and her ass, both of which were firm from running 6 miles a day. And then he started staring at her cleavage, natural double D's perched above an enviable tiny waist.

She laughed. "No thank you. I'm out of the biz. " She took a sip of her Bloody Mary, a perfect blend of Keitel One vodka, tomato juice, black pepper, Tabasco sauce and other secret ingredients she couldn't place. "But I'm in real trouble. I got gambling debts. I got a marker at a casino in Vegas, I'm not going to tell you which one, so don't ask me, but I got a marker. I got some Italian goombahs who have my number. If I want to live to see Christmas, I got to make some serious cash fast." This was the story she and Avery had cooked up to show why Regina would want to work for Carl. Sergei knew Regina was an investigator so he would naturally be suspicious if Regina asked to work for Carl. However, if she told him she had serious financial issues, so serious that she might lose her life because of them, it would almost make sense for her to work for Carl.

Sergei nodded. "Okay. So, you want to work for the Ivanov club, yes? Like I say, the girls age out at 25, but I would make an exception for a woman who looks like you. I think you may be very popular in that club."

She leaned forward, giving Sergei a good look at her large and surprisingly perky rack. She would have to seduce him in order for him to say yes. That turned her stomach because she hated manipulating men or anybody else, but it had to be done. He leaned forward as well, giving her a whiff of the cardamom, cinnamon, and absinthe in his high-dollar cologne.

"No. I don't want to work for that club," Regina said. "I'm interested in Carl Williams."

Sergei started to laugh. "Carl Williams? Regina, you could certainly pass for 25, so you could work for the Ivanov club, but, I'm sorry, with those breasts, no way you would be able to pass for under the age of 17. Nice try though."

Regina sighed. Did he really think she was going to try to pass for a child? How stupid did he think she was? She wanted to say, *no idiot, I'm talking about becoming a house mother.* But she decided to keep her calm. "No. I want to become one of the girl's house mothers. I know there's always about 20 girls living at the Williams compound and I know there is at least one house mother. Somebody who makes the girls feel comfortable, somebody they could look up to, and somebody who can gain the trust of runaway girls. I know Carl employs women for that role." It was important the house have a designated house mother, because, without one, the girls in the house tended to leave. They needed somebody to be their mother figure, because most of them didn't have a mother figure at their home, which was why they went to work for Carl in the first place. They hungered for an older woman to guide them.

Sergei shook his head. "Carl already has one of those. A house mother." Then he looked at her. "But you know, Regina, if I told Carl that you would do other services for his clientele – some of them want a real woman along with their children – he probably would hire you."

Regina sighed. Was this how it would be? Would she have to use herself as bait? She didn't know if she could go through with this. But then again, it was important that she do all she could to bring down this hell house.

She leaned back in her chair, thinking about how her feet hurt. *I can't wait to get home and get into a bathtub and take these damn shoes off.* How did women wear these shoes every day? If she lived to be 100, she would never understand why women put themselves through such agony just for fashion. She surreptitiously dangled one of the shoes off her feet and rubbed the arch.

Sergei was still watching her, an amused look on his face. "So should I tell Carl that you'll entertain his clients if he needs you to?"

Regina knew this might be the only way she could get this job. "Yeah. Tell him that." She would just have to find a way to get out of it once push came to shove because she wasn't doing it any more. Her days of being a sex worker were behind her and that was how she wanted it.

The waiter came around, refreshed both their drinks, and took their orders. Regina got the filet mignon with a baked potato and salad, while Sergei got the porterhouse with fries and the white truffle mac & cheese. Regina heard him ordering the white truffle mac & cheese, thought that sounded good, and changed her order from a salad to that. She wasn't on a diet, so why not live?

Sergei leaned forward giving her another whiff of his high-dollar cologne. "So, after this, you want to go to a smoky jazz club? Seven Grand is the place I like to hang out, but maybe you'd like to invite me to your place. Or maybe we can go to my place? My condo is on the water-front. I think you'd love it."

Regina would have to take a rain check on that. She didn't want him to get the wrong idea about what she was after. At the same time, she didn't want to insult him because she needed him. Without him serving as the link between her and Yuri, there was no way she could get a job in the Carl Williams circle. She would have to finesse it deli-cately, to say the very least.

"Let's just keep this friendly, okay? Sorry, man, I don't like to shit where I sleep."

She could tell that Sergei, being from Russia, wasn't familiar with that particular colloquialism. "What you mean, you don't like to shit where you sleep?"

"I mean I keep my business contacts strictly business, and my personal contacts strictly personal. You're a business relationship for me. Sorry, I don't want to bring sex into it."

She hoped that was good enough and he wasn't insulted by her turning him down. However, she could see in his face that wasn't the case. He looked disappointed, to say the very least. "I guess you don't want me to talk to Yuri after all, do you?"

She would have to throw something out there and hope that it did the trick. "Okay, the truth is I just don't like men." That wasn't really a lie. She didn't swing to women, although she had considered it a time or two in the past, but she also really didn't like men. At least, she didn't like men in the romantic sense. She had buddies, friends who were guys. A lot of guy friends. But that was as far as it went.

At first, Sergei looked stunned. Then he shook his head. "Oh, what a waste that is. To each his own, I guess." Then he got a wicked look on his face. "Or maybe I could watch some time?"

Don't push your luck, buddy. She decided to change the subject. That was just the easiest thing to do. "So, you seen any good movies lately?"

He got the hint. But she was still unsure that he would go to bat for her. She hoped he would but was shutting the whole romantic situation down, so she had no idea.

She just had to wait and see.

Chapter Three

TO REGINA'S RELIEF, Sergei apparently put a good word in for her, because she got a phone call from Yuri himself that Monday, asking her to come into his office for a formal interview. He wanted her to talk to both him and Carl and he wanted her to go to Carl's home in Del Mar.

So Regina got dressed up in a dress for the second time in four days. This was getting to be a bad habit, as far as she was concerned, but she knew that, just like with Sergei, Yuri would be a visual person. He would be more likely to hire her if she looked sexy. So, once again, she squeezed into the little black dress cut down to there and up to here and slipped on a pair of Christian Louboutin peep toes, the same black monstrosities that almost crippled her the night before.

Before she left, she emailed Christian, the lawyer who worked with Avery on the Esmeralda Gutierrez case. Christian was a very skilled computer hacker and Regina knew his skills would come in handy in the situation. She would have to find a way into Carl's computer system because she knew she would have to bring receipts in order for a court case to go forward.

"I'm headed over to Carl's, wish me luck," she texted him.

"Luck," was his one-worded text back to her.

Then she went out and got into her 10-year-old Prius and started down the road.

Del Mar was a seaside town, some 30 miles up the coast. Regina could get to Del Mar sometimes within an hour, if there was absolutely no traffic, but that was never the case in San Diego. Rush hour started around 6 in the morning and went all the way through 10 AM, Monday through Friday. In the evenings, it started at 3 and went through 7 o'clock. Especially on the Five, there was a lot of gridlocked traffic on the way up. Not that Regina cared about that – as an investigator, traffic was one thing she was used to, to say the very least. But it always sucked anyway.

She got to Carl's about an hour and half after she left her own house, seeing that it was 9:30. Her appointment time with Carl was at 9 AM. She cursed herself as she got to the long and winding driveway that led to Carl's compound. There was a guard standing by the enormous wrought-iron gate and she had to show him her driver's license before he would let her in the door.

"Go on in, Carl's expecting you," the armed guard told her without a smile. The guy was carrying an AR-15 and looked like somebody you didn't want to mess with.

So this is how it's going to be. The guy was obviously a control freak, not that she blamed him. After all, he was running an enormous pedophile ring. He really didn't have to be too afraid of getting prosecuted for what he was doing, and she still wanted to find out exactly why this was, but he obviously would take every precaution to make sure nobody knew what he was up to.

The house itself was about 10,000 square feet. It was perched on the edge of a cliff, and it was a modern design, all glass and angles. When she walked in, seeing the marble floor and 30 foot ceilings, she felt a bit out of place. This was definitely not her scene but she knew it was evidently the scene of a lot of people. She was astounded just a little that, in a place such as this, a billionaire's mansion, there could be such a house of horrors.

She was led to the back of the house where there was apparently an open-air office that looked out onto an enormous kidney-shaped pool. Carl stood up as she walked into his office. He looked her up and down appreciatively and held out his hand. "Carl Williams," he said as he shook her hand. "You must be Regina Baldwin. And this is Yuri Ivanov." He motioned to an older man sitting in an enormous leather wingback chair right next to Carl's 10-foot glass desk. "Please, take a seat."

Carl was a handsome guy, about 60, in good shape, and looked 20 years younger. He was tall and slim with elegant fingers. His face was angular with a sharp nose and jawline. He had an amazing set of choppers, the best money could buy. They were white and straight and his smile was disarming. He spoke in clipped tones that indicated to Regina that he was from a different country, probably either Australia or England. Yuri, on the other hand, was around 70, with white hair and a weathered face. However, like Carl, he had taken good care of himself over the years. He didn't smile when she walked in. Neither did he look her up and down, like Carl did.

Regina was a master at reading people. It was obvious

that Carl was the one with the salacious appetite. He made no pretense about that. He looked like he wanted to devour her on the spot, undressing her with his eyes. On the other hand, Yuri appeared to be all business. He had a notepad in his hand and he barely looked at her as she sat down next to him.

After Regina sat down, she looked past Carl at the view below her. The Pacific Ocean was rolling in about 50 feet below the house. It was a clear day, blue skies and warm, and she had a sudden urgency to leave this place and get to where she felt comfortable. This gorgeous home, with its 30 foot ceilings, marble and hardwood floors, and its magnificent view, nevertheless had a certain vibe about it. In her ears, she could imagine the cries of desperate young girls tricked into a monstrous sexual servitude. She knew she wasn't really hearing these cries, it was only in her head, but that was the kind of vibe she was getting from this beautiful home.

Yet she would have to put on her game face and pretend she was all-in with this situation.

"Now I understand that, from Sergei, you're interested in procuring girls for my clientele," Carl said. "And that you are also interested in the role of house mother. I can assure you that we have one of those. Her name is Jacqueline and she's been with us five years. So I'm very sorry, but, at the moment, I don't have an opening for the position you want."

Regina bit her lower lip. Obviously, this guy called her for some reason. She shuddered to think what that reason was. "So am I wasting my time here?" She looked at the two men. Yuri didn't look at her but Carl smiled.

He made a steeple with his hands. "I'm looking to

expand my stable a bit. I cater to a clientele that has very particular tastes. Very singular tastes. I'm sure you know what they are – Sergei has explained to you the people I manage here. All my girls are of a certain age group. They're all clean, they're checked every single day, and they all have a certain *je ne sais quoi*. The clientele I attract are some of the most wealthy and powerful men in the world. They know I'm discreet, can provide them with what they hunger for, and they pay very good money for the privilege of accessing the girls I procure."

The way he was talking, it all seemed so… sterile. She knew the reality of the situation, and that was that he was trafficking very young girls. She wondered exactly who he was talking about when he said that he was catering to some of the most wealthy and powerful people in the world.

He continued on. "My clientele ranges from high-level politicians, to heads of industry, to famous actors and celebrities, to high-level athletes. You have to understand, the membership at this club starts at $50,000 per month. Only the singular gentlemen with singular tastes would be interested in this arrangement. The memberships run year-to-year and some members take advantage of the lovely ladies on a weekly basis, while others come a few times a year. Everybody leaves satisfied, however, of that I can assure you."

"When you say high-level politicians, who exactly are you talking about?"

"Heads of state. Both former and current. We've hosted quite a few prime ministers from overseas. When they come to visit the United States, this is a destination for them. In the United States, we typically see senators, governors, both current and former. My girls need somebody to guide them in the ways of the upper crust. We have a doyenne who works with the girl on their manners, ways of speaking, the words they are supposed to use with high-level individuals. She's very good. She lives here as well. The girls who service my clientele live in the guesthouse on the grounds. There are about 20 girls who stay here at any given time."

Regina took a deep breath. She had a feeling this entire thing was over her head. While she intellectually knew this ring was catering to high profile individuals, she didn't imagine the kinds of people who would be taking part of this sick charade were people at the highest level of government. It would be very difficult to take this ring down, to say the very least.

A thought crossed her mind. Becky was murdered some 20 years ago. She was a part of this ring. What if she was murdered because she was going to tell somebody about what was going on? What if that's what they did to any girls who tried to get out of line? If that was the case, who would ensure her own safety, let alone the safety of the girls she would try to persuade to be used for her own case? Would she be endangering the lives of the girls she would try to talk into being a part of the lawsuit she and Avery were planning? Would she be endangering her own life?

She felt a little nauseated but would have to feel her way around. She would have to come up with a foolproof plan, nothing half-assed here. "Okay. So, you were saying?"

"Yes. I was saying that I was looking to expand my appeal. Now as I said, I have a very singular operation here. I could tell you that there is no other operation like mine in the world, but I would be lying. There are other ones, all top-secret, mainly in different countries, but there is one other one in the United States. In Florida. I obviously do not offer women who can be procured at any high-class hotel in any big city. My girls are very young. But I get many requests from men who want to take part in my services and want to share in the fun that a party at this home can bring, but don't necessarily want to take part in the usual fare. They want a woman who's a bit older, sophisticated, and stunningly gorgeous. Sergei surreptitiously took a picture of you with a cell phone and I knew you would fit the bill beautifully. He also told me you have experience. So I would like you to be a part of my stable here."

Stable. Stable is a place where you keep animals. That's all these girls are to him. Animals. Chattel. Property. They're to be used and discarded like yesterday's trash.

Regina sat up higher in her chair and took a deep breath. She would have to accept this position and would have to do what this guy wanted. At least until she could figure out her way around this place and figure out how to get at least five girls on her side. That would be an impossible task.

She finally just shook her head. "I'm very sorry, but I'm going to have to decline your invitation. I might have been a hooker in my prior life but I'm not anymore. However, I do need money, I won't lie. But I guess I'm going to have to look in a different place for what I need."

She had a feeling he would call her bluff. It was obvious this guy wanted her in more ways than one. She felt the kind of power over him, could feel she was drawing him in. She could never understand why so many men thought with their pecker, but this guy obviously was at the moment.

"Okay. Perhaps we could do this. We need a hostess for our parties. As I said, the girls I have around this compound are very young. Many of them don't really know how to socialize on the high-level I command. As I told you before, we have a doyenne working with them, but the men who attend these parties sometimes need a little more of an adult stimulation. I would like you to join my elite group. You would not have to offer sexual favors to the men who attend my parties but I would like you to be at the parties. Mingle. Talk to the men, give them some kind of adult conversation they won't be getting from the younger girls who will be servicing them later. Would you be interested in something like that?"

Regina felt an inward sigh of relief. "Yes. I would like to do something like that. Although I have a feeling it won't be paying as much as if I were to sexually satisfy your guests."

"You're right about that, of course. I could certainly get top dollar for you if you would give my men the services they would desire from you. But I want you on my team. I can pay you $1,000 per week and all you have to do is show up at my parties five evenings a week. You can even work your regular job." He smiled. "Thank of this as a part-time gig. A side hustle, as it were."

Regina nodded. That sounded good to her. *A side hustle. Interesting choice of words for being the maitre d' of a pedophilia ring.* "When do I start?" Regina asked.

"Tonight would be fine." He raised an eyebrow. "You were prepared to start right away, were you not?"

"Yes." Regina was mentally rubbing her hands together. "That would be fine."

She shook hands with the two men and then promptly left, after Carl informed her that she was to be back at his palace at 8 PM sharp. Apparently, this party would get started late because sometimes the parties would start early, at around 5 or 6, and would end early as well. Those earlier parties took place when Carl would have to be up early to catch a flight to Japan, Europe or Australia. This wasn't the case, so Carl scheduled this party to go on late into the night.

Regina stopped by the pool area before leaving for the day. She had investigations to do for a variety of attorneys and had to meet with Avery to tell her about her new position.

While she was out there, she saw a young guy sitting out by the pool already. He was sitting on a lounge chair, his eyes covered with reflective sunglasses. He had curly hair, bow-shaped lips and the same strong jawline as Carl. His body was lean, buff and tan. He smiled as she walked next to the beautiful kidney-shaped pool and 15-person hot tub that bubbled in the corner.

"Nice, huh?" the guy said with a smile.

"Yeah," Regina said. She was thinking it was a nice place as far as physical beauty. Undeniably. In the middle of a pool was a bar where you could swim up to and get cocktails to drink while you floated along. There was even a bartender at the ready, even though nobody was around to keep the guy busy. Nobody but this kid, whoever he was. As beautiful as this place was, however, she felt it was tainted by the degradation this place represented.

The kid lifted his glasses and Regina realized he wasn't a kid at all. He was around her age. She must have just assumed he was a kid because he was lounging around the pool in the middle of the day instead of working a job like the rest of the world.

He stood up and shook her hand, a towering figure with a firm handshake. "I'm Jurgen Williams," he said. "Carl's son."

"Regina Baldwin," she said. "I'm, uh, going to be working for your dad." It suddenly made sense about why this guy was lounging around the pool on a Tuesday afternoon. He probably didn't have a job. He probably just lived off his daddy's money. He looked like a rich trust fund baby who didn't know the meaning of an honest day's work.

"Oh?" he said, suddenly frowning. "What will you be doing for him?"

"I guess I'm going to be a hostess with the mostest for awhile. You know, walk around the parties, fluffing the old dudes before they get down and dirty with…" Regina didn't want to say it. She saw in Jurgen's eyes that he knew what she was unable to say. Which meant he knew about his father's "side hustle." As far as Regina was concerned, that was all she needed to know about Jurgen. Anybody who would stand idly by while all this was going on wasn't a person who Regina wanted to know.

"Yeah," Jurgen said, bowing his head. "I guess I don't really want to know. I was thinking you would be working for his legitimate business. That's what I do. I work for his hedge fund business."

"Oh? And what are you doing here, lounging around on a Tuesday afternoon?" Regina asked.

"I have a meeting with my father in an hour. I was about to get into the shower before meeting with him. Then you showed up, and, well, I'm talking to you. But I have to get going. My dad gets mad when I'm even a little bit late."

He smiled and Regina, in spite of herself, smiled back. "Your dad. What he does here. What do you think about that?" Regina asked, suddenly getting a kernel of an idea.

His smile disappeared. "I compartmentalize," he said. "I can't even think about all of that. If I did, I would probably try to kill my old man. So I try not to think about what goes on here."

Regina didn't know if she could believe him or not. He

seemed sincere, but, at the same time, there was something just a little off about him.

She looked around at the statues in the corner of the pool area, the Bougainvillea flowers that grew in hedges to make the entire area much more private, at the little tiki bar in the middle of the pool that had a bartender just waiting to take orders, and she pictured the parties she would be hosting. She imagined the flabby old men leering at the nubile young girls, who no doubt were disgusted by the men but nonetheless knew what they had to do with these old coots. She would be a part of this life, starting that evening, but, with any luck, she would get out soon.

"So yeah, what do you do? When you know about what your father does with these girls?"

He shrugged. "What can I do? I mean, seriously, I'm sure I'm not the first guy disgusted by his father and I know I won't be the last. Father employs me and pays me very well."

So this guy can be bought. Regina had little respect for people who were blackmailed into doing horrendous things. She had no respect for people bribed to do these things.

"You have a nice life," Regina said. *I hope you can look at yourself in the mirror every day.*

Jurgen looked askance at Regina. "If I didn't know better, I would think you were judging me." He folded his arms. "You *are* judging me."

Regina finally took a deep breath. It wasn't in her interest to let this guy know what her game was. "Who am I to be judging anybody? After all, I'm going to start working for the bastard, starting tonight."

Jurgen just smiled at her. "Why do I think you have some kind of ulterior motive? If you do, your secret is safe with me."

Regina didn't trust him, although she had a good feeling that he might be somebody useful to her in the future. She would have to get to know the guy, maybe put him in her back pocket. He was the ultimate insider.

Then again, if he had not been turned by now, maybe he never would be.

Chapter Four

THAT EVENING, Regina showed back up at the compound. A party was in full swing and she just observed everything. She was very careful that when Carl would come out to the pool area, which was where the party was going, she would actively pretend to do her hostess duties. She would start talking to the men, most of whom were over the age of 60 with flabby middles and sunken chests, but whenever Carl wasn't around, she would take a seat on the edge of the pool area and just watch everybody.

She would have to make friends with the girls and see who was the weak link of the bunch. The one most likely to turn on this whole organization. The girls no doubt had different motivations for doing what they were doing. All of them were being exploited, but at the same time, she knew these girls had reasons for being there. Maybe some of them had issues with self-esteem, maybe some of them had family issues, maybe some had families in financial dire straits. She thought most of the girls were runaways, so were like she was at one time – they needed someone to take care of them and Carl promised just that for them. Maybe some of them were looking to be part of a family, and since the girls were living dormitory-style in Carl's guesthouse, they probably were a support system for one another. For now, however, she was just observing.

She noticed one person different from all the others. He was a tall, slender man, with sandy blonde hair styled in a slight pompadour on top. He wasn't in a swimming suit, even though he was next to the pool. He was dressed in a light pink button-down that was open, a white T-shirt under that, baggy khaki pants and leather boots. He wasn't drinking alcohol. And, like her, he seemed to just be observing the scene.

Regina was curious about this guy. He was definitely a man set apart from the others. The other men were frolicking in the pool, hitting on all the girls, and, much to Regina's disgust, all of the other men at this party disappeared with one girl after another for hours at a time. But not this guy. He was just casually sitting in his lounge chair, taking everything in.

She caught his eye and he lifted his cup of water towards her and nodded. She just smiled and looked away.

The house mother living there and looking after the girls was named Jacqueline Price. She was about 35 years old, and, from what Regina understood, had been in the business her entire adult life. She had previously worked in underground clubs like the Ivanov club. But she had explained to Regina that she had aged out of these clubs, so now she did this job. She saw it as grooming the younger generation. Regina thought that was a sick way of looking at it but she wasn't going to let on that she was thinking that. Jacqueline might be valuable to her because she could confide in her about the girls and what they might be going through.

For now, however, Regina had to know about the mysterious man with the sandy blonde hair who appeared to be on the outside of everything.

Jacqueline was sitting on a lounge chair, talking to one girl after another who had come up to her to ask her about this guy or that. She gave each girl an encouraging word before sending them on their way.

Regina went over to her. "Hey. What's with that guy over there?" She motioned her head over to the guy sitting on the lounge chair, observing everybody.

Jacqueline shrugged. "He's a looky-loo. Name's Jackson Eisel."

"What do you mean by that?"

"I mean that he likes to observe, not play. That's okay. When he joined this club, he told Carl that he was more of a voyeur and didn't like to actually partake in the same things everybody else was doing. He pays his dues just like everybody else so Carl doesn't mind him."

Regina looked over at the guy and she had her doubts that he was a voyeur. He just didn't seem the type.

"Is he here a lot?" Regina asked.

"Enough. Why do you ask?"

"No reason."

She would have to keep her eye on this guy.

Chapter Five

SEVERAL WEEKS WENT by and Regina was slowly getting to know the girls in the house. There was Britney, age 14, who was escaping an abusive father. Britney was from New York City and Regina learned that she had run away from home and somehow managed to get enough money for a bus ticket out here. She'd heard that San Diego was a tropical paradise and she always loved the beach. She'd been homeless for several weeks because she didn't know how to get any kind of social services. She was at a bus station, sleeping, when Jacqueline found her and brought her here. She confided in Regina, telling her she didn't like what she was doing but didn't really see any options.

Her story was fairly typical. Girls at this place came from all over the nation. Most of them were escaping neglectful and abusive situations, just like Britney. Regina heard quite a few tales of girls raped by their stepfathers or their own fathers. One girl, Celeste, told Regina that her father got her pregnant. She got an abortion and then just disappeared onto the streets of Toledo, Ohio. She was found by a man by the name of Oleg Petrenko and he brought her to San Diego to work for Carl. Regina knew that Oleg Petrenko was a member of the Ivanov clan and the Ivanovs were working hand in glove with Carl.

Those were the stories that broke Regina's heart. But the ones that really upset her were the girls who explained to Regina that they were there because their own mothers had sent them there.

"My dad, he's like this millionaire," Emma, age 14, explained to Regina. "And, like, he left our family a couple years ago. And, like, it turned out he was like stealing from his company. And stealing from a bunch of people. And, like, the feds came and got him and put him into jail. And my mom, she don't have any kind of skills to make money, and we have this house in La Jolla. Like, my mom, she don't want to lose her house. So she found me this job."

When Regina heard this, she wanted to find that girl's mother and strangle her. If your husband leaves you in the lurch, you don't send your child into prostitution. You move into a small apartment and take whatever job you can get. But it sounded like this mother wasn't going to give up her lifestyle, no matter what, and Regina saw red about the whole situation.

Worse still, Emma's story wasn't even all that unusual. Other girls also came to work for Carl at the behest of their mother or sometimes their father. She could never picture ever doing something like that to a child of hers.

She was also slowly starting to understand the arrangement Carl had with the prosecutors and the police in town. It wasn't just that a lot of money changed hands, although that was true enough. But it was also that the Ivanovs owned certain prosecutors and policemen. The Ivanov family was very good at finding incriminating materials to blackmail just about everybody in town. They employed a team of computer hackers who were able to find any kind of skeleton that any judge, policeman, or prosecutor would have in their closet. They knew all the corrupt actions that their judges, prosecutors, and policeman were undergoing. They knew who was dirty. They knew everybody down-loading child pornography, everybody accepting bribes, everybody with a drug problem. And if anybody who they wanted on their team was squeaky clean, with nothing in their background that could make them vulnerable to being compromised, the Ivanovs made sure to set them up. It wasn't unusual for the Ivanovs to follow a prosecutor to Vegas, put something in that prosecutor's drink, plant a child in their bed, and take pictures.

Regina even heard a tale of a dead hooker being planted in a policeman's bed, just like in the movie *The Godfather Part Two*.

One thing was for sure, the Ivanovs were ruthless and they always got what they wanted, which was to get kompromat on everybody and anybody who might try to bring them down.

And then, one evening, Regina saw something that really made her want to cut a bitch.

Paul Sharpton was attending one of the parties.

Chapter Six

REGINA WAS KEEPING me apprised about everything going on over at the Carl Williams compound. She and I were slowly starting to put our plan together, and, at the same time, I was trying to figure out a way around the whole immunity-from-prosecution angle. I lost hope when Regina explained to me exactly how entangled the prosecutors, cops and judges were with the Ivanov family. I would have to go with my other plan as far as bringing down the Carl Williams organization. The only thing that would work was a lawsuit brought by the girls. Regina was working on that.

But Regina had something else she had to tell me. She was very excited one evening, after one of the parties. "Can I come by?" she asked me.

It was 10 o'clock at night but I was still working on one of my cases. I'd brought work home, as usual, because my dance card was full after my big win in the Esme Gutierrez case. People were pounding down my door and I was able to pick and choose the cases I really believed in.

This was definitely one of them.

"Sure. I'll probably be up until at least 1 o'clock in the morning." I was still having problems with insomnia and these problems had not abated at all. I was still seeing my therapist about it but she didn't know what to do for me. She tried to instruct me about how to do guided meditation and yoga and she prescribed some herbs. I even tried hypnotism. But I still was only getting about four hours of sleep a night.

I petted Lola and Harlow, both of whom were snoring next to me on the balcony, which was where I brought my work. It was a nice evening, with a beautiful breeze. Clear and bright, even though I knew winter was coming and with it came much chillier nights. Especially here on the coast.

Aidan was out for the evening. He had just taken his bar exam and passed it on the first try, bless his heart. I was very proud of him because I knew the California bar wasn't the easiest one to pass. He'd started working for the personal injury firm, Pierce and Wright, working on class-action lawsuits. He was also continuing on his work with the wrongfully detained mental patients, which was work he had come to know and love.

I thought Aidan had an affinity for people with mental problems because our father had recently been diagnosed with bipolar disorder. That fit. I always thought our father was a little bit off. When he was up, he was very up. When I was little, before he left, he used to stay up late at night, cooking, writing and painting. He would throw manic puppet shows for Aidan and me, which made both of us laugh.

But our father also had a dark side. He would throw tantrums at very random times, screaming at my mother, me and Aidan, about a dish being a little bit dirty or about the dog peeing in the house. He would shut himself in his room for weeks at a time, hardly coming out. Because of this, he worked only sporadically unless he could possibly find a job where he didn't have to leave the house. He managed to find just such a job, but it was doing surveys online, so it didn't pay very much at all. That was part of why my mother and I were so poor - my father couldn't send his child support because he didn't work very much.

When my father finally got his diagnosis of bi-polar disorder, it was a relief for everybody. He was finally taking some meds and I had hope that maybe, just maybe, he would finally get his act together and get a job and a real life.

At any rate, Aidan had a lot of sympathy for him and that was why he enjoyed working with the mental patients. He told me that he always wanted to help our dad but never could, so he wanted to help these people instead.

———

REGINA GOT to my apartment at 11 o'clock. She was smiling, the first real smile I'd seen on her face in a while. She had a bottle of scotch in her hand and two rocks glasses.

She came out onto the balcony, looking at the work I had spread in front of me, and informed me it was time to put this work away because we were going to celebrate.

I was very curious about what she wanted to celebrate.

"You'll find out." She poured me a glass of scotch and herself as well. "Okay. Here's the deal." She took a sip of the scotch and so did I. It was dry, woody and smooth. "Damn that's good. Anyhow, here's the deal. Your prosecutor, Paul Sharpton, is a freak. He's a nasty freak, because he was at the party tonight and was getting down and dirty with the girls."

"Are you sure?"

"Absolutely positive." I'd shown Regina pictures of Paul, so she knew exactly what he looked like. The beauty of it was that he didn't know her. Even though she was working for a lot of other attorneys in the area, she worked behind the scenes. Paul wouldn't necessarily recognize her if she was at a party.

I bit my lower lip, thinking about what that meant.

"Here's the thing," Regina said. "I did my investigation of Paul and I didn't find anything on him. I had Christian hack his computer and I didn't find anything that made me think he was dirty. I was trying to figure out exactly why he'd be so willing to throw you under the bus like that. Now I know. He apparently wants to get his freak on with these children. He wants to do this in the privacy of Carl's compound and he knows anybody else who's there who might see him would also have something up their sleeve. You know, you see somebody at a sex club, you're not necessarily going to tell anybody about it, because why were you there in the first place? So yeah, this guy's dirty as hell."

"Okay. So he's dirty. And what do you mean, he was getting down and dirty with the girls?"

"This is what happens at these parties. I've gone to enough of them that I know the score. The game. Everybody kind of meets each other at these parties. Sometimes the parties are out by the pool, sometimes they're inside, but the whole point of these parties is that they're meet and greets. These old geezers are there for one reason and one reason only – to meet these kids. And that's what they are, kids. Everybody starts talking, and then, one by one, an old coot will disappear with a young girl, and come back out, find another girl, and then disappear with her. Sometimes a single old perv will disappear with three or four girls in the same night. That's what I saw Paul do. He disappeared with two different girls over the course of the night. I saw him do it."

I folded my arms. "That makes sense. I've always wondered why he moved out here right after my trial. It fits - perhaps Carl promised him a lifetime membership or something in exchange for him railroading me into prison." I took another sip of my scotch. "Now how can we use this information?"

"Here's the beauty of it all. Paul was drinking a lot, and, trust me, I was on him like white on rice all night. I was trying to figure out if he'd say something that might give me some kind of information we could use. Because you're right, just the fact that he's a client of this Carl person doesn't necessarily give us a way to bring them down. However, I heard him say something that made me sit up and take notice."

"What was that?" I asked her.

"He has a brother named Max. The child he was talking to was asking if he wanted to take pictures of her in the nude. He was saying he wanted to do that. Then he told her that he liked to take pictures of girls like her but he used his brother Max's computer to store them. Then I figured out why he was doing that to his brother. Max is in prison for drug possession."

"In prison for drug possession? I don't understand. Paul's a prosecutor. Drug possession is a minor crime. I wonder why Paul didn't use his influence to keep his brother out of prison for something like that? What kind of drugs did he possess, did he say?"

Regina was shaking her head. "You don't get it, do you?

Here's what I'm thinking happened. Paul wanted his brother to go to prison because he wanted to use his brother's computer, his passwords, his security firewalls, everything, because he wanted to have all these child porn images but didn't want them on his own computer. So he throws Max in the clink and commandeers Max's computer for his dirty deeds. He makes sure that Max goes to prison for something relatively minor, uses Max's computer to put his child porn on, and, if the feds ever raid, he has plausible deniability. It's ingenious, really. Completely psychotic and royally fucked up but ingenious."

"So let's put together a plan to bring this guy down," I said. "Obviously, the first thing we're going to have to do is find the brother in prison. He probably has no idea what his brother Paul is doing. Because, you know, if the FBI does a sting, he'll be on the hook, not his sleazy brother Paul."

Then again, that didn't really make sense, either. Max was in prison. The images Paul put on Max's computer had to have been time-stamped. It would seem that Max would have an airtight alibi for these images if anybody ever deigned to raid. But it would also be difficult to show Paul was the culprit.

It was then that I got an idea about how I would prove that Paul was downloading the images onto Max's computer.

Chapter Seven

I FOUND MAX EASILY ENOUGH. He was serving time in the federal prison in Bakersfield. He was fortunate enough to be serving time in a minimum security prison so there wasn't fencing around the building, the housing was dormitory style, and the emphasis was on work and program orientations. I knew he was serving time for possession of cocaine with intent to distribute, in that he had more than an ounce on his person at the time of the raid.

I found out that Max was working for a tobacco shop that was a front for a drug operation in the back, and, according to the statement of information in his file, he insisted he had no idea drugs were back there. From what I gathered about his case, it seemed as if his brother wanted him to be put away but his brother also wanted him to not have to suffer too much, which was why he was in a minimum security prison. I knew something about federal prisons and the prison he was in was really more of a Club Fed. The inmates weren't violent - they were mainly white-collar criminals serving time for tax evasion, embezzlement, perjury and the like. There were a few people in there for drug possession but not as many who were in there for possession with intent to distribute, as was the case with Max.

I went to the penitentiary, told the guard who I was seeing, and because it was during visiting hours, it wasn't a problem getting a chance to talk with him. I was able to speak with him one-on-one because I was an attorney and also because that was apparently how the prisoners in this place took their visits. There was a large room with tables all around and I got a chance to sit there and wait for him to see me.

———

MAX CAME OUT ABOUT HALF an hour after I got there. He was dressed in a light beige jumpsuit, his dark wavy hair appeared to be freshly cut, and he was clean-shaven. He was a nice-looking guy, as was his brother, even though his brother, to me, was amazingly sleazy. Max looked to be about my age. Paul was probably in his early 40s, because I knew he was around 25 when he prosecuted my case. I was one of the first murder trials he prosecuted.

I stood up when Max came out and held out my hand. He shook it, looking very confused as to why I was there.

"Max, my name is Avery Collins. I'm an attorney. Thank you very much for meeting me."

We both sat down. "Of course I'm going to meet you, what else am I going to do? I was told I had a visitor. That's all I know. Now you say you're an attorney? I guess I don't understand. I'm all out of appeals. I'm serving time here for the next five years and I really don't understand why you're here."

"I'm here because I needed to ask you a few questions about your brother Paul."

He shook his head. "I don't want to talk about Paul. Paul screwed me over. Big time. You say I have a brother named Paul. I say I don't have a brother named Paul anymore. In fact, I have no brothers at all. I have a couple of sisters, however. Eileen and Nora. Identical twins, younger than me, they come and visit me all the time. But Paul, he don't visit me because he knows what he did."

"What did Paul do?"

"How long you got? Never mind, I only have about a half-hour to speak with you anyway. At least that's what the guard told me."

I looked at my watch. "Okay. Then let's get rolling. I took a look at your file and I see you were working for a head shop selling tobacco products and marijuana paraphernalia, and, in the back, they were selling cocaine. How did you come to work for this place?"

He leaned forward a little bit. His hands weren't handcuffed and he clasped them in front of him. "My brother Paul. Oh, sorry, my former brother, Paul, got me the job. He told me to work for this guy, Harry." He shook his head. "Only Harry, he didn't get charged in this case. He was the one dealing drugs. He never told me about it. I had no idea. The drugs were in a locked closet in the back of the store. I didn't have keys to the closet and Harry never let me open it. I had no idea there were drugs back there but here comes the feds, questioning me after hours."

"Who tipped the feds off about what was going on?" I had a feeling it was Paul himself who tipped the feds off and I had a strong feeling that Harry wasn't prosecuted because Paul made sure Harry wasn't prosecuted. It was evidently a sting operation and Paul must've had some kind of pull in the prosecutor's office to make sure Harry himself wasn't prosecuted for this crime.

"I never did find out. It was an anonymous tip. Anyhow, they threw the book at me. Five years in prison for something I didn't do. But my brother, he must've pulled some strings and got me here, so there's that. At least I'm not serving time in some maximum-security hellhole. Small graces, as they preach to us here in church."

"Okay. You said you got five years in prison for something you didn't do. And yet you just told me that you're to be here for the next five years. You've already served five years. How did you get your time extended?"

"I caught a new case. My brother came to me one day and told me our mother was dying and wanted to see me. I couldn't get a furlough to see her so I just left. I hitchhiked my way back to San Diego and went to my mother's house to find out that she was just fine. I mean, I'm glad she's fine and all. But I had no idea why Paul would've said that to me if she was perfectly healthy. I hitchhiked back to the prison and I was in trouble. I had a trial about my, what I call self-furlough, because it's bullshit I couldn't get a real one, and they extended my sentence by five years. So that's why I'm in here for another five years."

"You mean, even after you broke out of prison, they put you back here in minimum-security?" That didn't make any sense to me. Usually when people break out of minimum security prisons – and it's relatively easy to do, because there's no fence around the perimeter – they don't come back to the minimum-security prison. They go to a higher security place. But this guy was able to come back here?

"Yeah. I guess that was my brother pulling the strings again. I don't know exactly how he's able to pull all these strings but I'm glad for it." He swept his hands around the room. "This place, it ain't too bad. They have concerts outside every Friday night, there's a rec center where guys play pool, foosball and ping-pong, and guys play basketball, football and all kinds of things out in the courtyard. There's any kind of drugs you want in here, but I don't get into that kind of thing. Some of the female guards even give action to the inmates around here. The guys here, they're not bad. Not bad at all." He leaned forward. "I even see some guys who are kind of celebrities. You know, they get pinched for not paying their taxes and whatnot and there they are. I hear that even Tommy Chong was housed here one time, man."

Suddenly, the picture was becoming very clear to me. His brother set him up to break out of prison by telling him his mother was dying. He set him up by sending him to work for Harry in the first place. And yet, Paul had enough decency to make sure his brother served time in Club Fed. There was no way in hell that, after he broke out of this place, he'd just be brought back here.

Obviously Paul was able to pull strings and I was going to have to find out exactly how he could do that. He must've had an arrangement with a judge. I looked through the file, saw the judge for his absconding case and the underlying drug case was Judge Cooper, and I knew I would have to look into some kind of arrangement Judge Cooper had with Paul.

"Okay. So, let me tell you why I'm here. And I think it's important you know this. But your brother, the reason he put you in here, I believe, is because he wants to use your computer to download child porn."

He cocked his head. "I don't understand. What do you mean?"

"You have a home and you own it, right?"

He nodded. "Yeah. My Aunt Genevieve left me her home in her will. My brother makes sure the taxes are paid each year, but, other than that, I think my house has been vacant all these years. I asked my brother to rent it out but he hasn't done that."

"And in this home is a computer, right?"

He had to think about that one for a second. "Yes. Yes, I had a computer. But it's been five years. You mean to tell me that computer's still going after all these years?"

"I don't know. Actually, it would be perfect if there was a new computer in there that's being used, because that would be one way to nab your brother at what he's doing. Anyhow, your brother is most likely using your computer. That's probably why you're in prison in the first place."

Max looked confused. "You think he arranged for me to go to prison just because he wanted to use my computer? I guess I don't understand."

"Here's the thing. Your brother evidently has a problem with pedophilia. He regularly attends a party where very young girls service older men, like your brother. He obviously can't have a computer in his home and access child porn. If the FBI ever came and raided him, he'd go to prison for a long time, and, trust me, the prison he'd go to wouldn't be as nice as this one. He'd go to a very bad place, probably for the rest of his life."

It was just dawning on Max that his brother was probably just diabolical enough to do that to him.

"So he goes to my house and does his thing?"

"Yes. Did you have broadband Internet before you went to prison?"

"Yeah. Paul wanted me to get broadband. He set it up for me. I don't like to deal with things like that." He shook his head. "Wait a minute. You mean nobody ever canceled the Internet?"

"I doubt it but I'm going to have to find out for sure. Did you ask Paul to cancel your Internet?"

"Yes, I did, as a matter of fact. I asked Paul to take care of my affairs for me while I'm gone. I asked him to pay my property taxes on my house, make sure the lawn is mowed, look after the house, and shut off all my utilities, including my Internet. Are you telling me he didn't cancel my utilities and my Internet?"

"No. I'm not telling you that until I know for sure. But I have a reasonable suspicion that your utilities are still active and so is your Internet. You had it set up for automatic debit, right? How much money was in your bank account when you came into prison?"

"About $50,000. My aunt left me that money too. What can I say, I was her favorite. So yeah, there was plenty of money in my checking account to pay any kind of utilities and Internet for quite a few years." He put his hand to his temple and massaged it. "But come on now. If my brother doesn't shut everything off, I won't have anything in the bank when I get out."

"I'm just telling you my suspicions. I'm going to have to get your signature on this power of attorney so I can legitimately look into your utility and Internet bills. And I also need your signature on this piece of paper that'll give me access to your home. I'd like to see if there's a computer in your home, and if there is, I'd like to have it forensically analyzed. Can I do that? Will you sign these documents that'll allow me to do those things?"

He still looked confused but nodded. "Yeah. There's a notary here because guys have to sign and notarize documents all the time. I'll talk to my supervisor. But yeah, sure, you can go into my house. I don't have the keys to my house, of course, but you'll be able to get a locksmith to help you get in, right?"

"Yes. I also want to have the computer analyzed for any kind of DNA on it. That's also part of the permission you're giving me."

He went up and got his supervisor, and then the two of us went into an office where there was a notary. Max looked over the documents I gave to him and signed them.

"I really hope you can get to the bottom of this. Because if my brother really was setting me up, then that's some bullshit right there. I mean, it's not a bad life back here. It's not like I'm really suffering. But I'm going to be getting out of prison at some point and I'm going to be coming out as a felon. I have no idea who's going to hire me. Not to mention that I'm missing out on life back here. If my brother was responsible for putting me here, just because he wanted to go to my house and use my computer to get his perverted freak on, then that's all kind of messed up."

"You said you were angry with him, even before you found out he's probably setting you up. Why are you so angry with him?"

"Because. He was in the prosecutor's office when I got busted for this. He didn't speak up for me. In fact, he testified against me. He told the court that I told him I knew about those drugs being in the back of that head shop. He's why I'm here in the first place. He lied about me in a court of law, but I didn't think he would've done all that just because he wanted to use my computer."

"After all that," I began. "Why did you trust him to pay your property taxes on your home and take care of your Internet and utility bills?"

He shrugged. "I needed someone to do it and he offered

it. And that's it. I could've asked my sisters to do it, but Paul offered first and I took him up on it. There's really nothing more than that. I guess I was just naïve, thinking he was going to actually do those things. I mean, I guess he's been paying my property taxes and good for him. But if things are like you say, I guess he wasn't shutting off my utilities and Internet like he said he was going to."

No, it's safe to say that he didn't do those things. "Okay. So. I'm going to do a few things and I'll come back and see you in a couple of weeks. I'll let you know what I found out."

"Thanks. I knew my brother was a shady person. I had no idea just how shady he really is."

I knew Paul was shady. I knew it when he prosecuted me and withheld evidence.

But I was about to find out just how shady he really was.

Chapter Eight

I WENT DOWN to Christian's office the next day because I wanted him to be a part of the situation. He was able to hack into any computer I found on Max's property, no problem. But, at the same time, I wanted this to be done correctly. It would be the only way I'd be able to get the kind of leverage I'd be looking for with Paul. And leverage would be the only way to see justice done in the Carl Williams' case.

I knocked lightly on his open door. He was sitting behind his desk, working on his computer. I was proud of him. Ever since he'd started his private practice, and especially because he was my second chair in the Esme Gutierrez case, people had been banging down his door, wanting to hire him as their attorney.

"Hey, Avery, what's up?"

"I wanted to see if you wanted to do some field work with me. I'm going over to this guy's house. His name is Max Sharpton. Paul Sharpton's brother. He's in prison because Paul put him there. Anyhow, I have a strong suspicion that Paul Sharpton has been going over to Max's house and downloading kiddie porn. I was kind of hoping that maybe you would go along with me to Max's house? I don't know, I'm a little bit nervous about it."

"What do you want me to do?"

"Find out if there's some kind of a security system and remotely shut it down. Also, I don't know how good you are at breaking into homes. I mean, it's not really breaking in, because the guy that owns a home has given me permission to go onto the premises. But I have a feeling the cops will come anyway and I just want to do as little explaining as possible. I hope that makes sense."

Christian grinned. "Of course I'll help you. Once we get about 10 feet away from the home, I can figure out if he has a wireless security system that relies on radiofrequency signals. A lot of these home monitoring systems fail to encrypt or authenticate signals being sent from the sensors to the control panels, so all I have to do is intercept the data, decipher the commands, and play them back to the control panels."

He was talking Greek to me, but I knew that he could disable the security system. Then it would just be a matter of the two of us jamming our way into the house.

"How good are you at picking locks?" I asked him.

"Pretty damn good." He smiled again. "So I'm assuming you don't want to do this the legit way?"

"Not really. I mean, I have a document that states I have permission to be on the premises, but I know those lock-smiths get really sticky about these kinds of things. Not too many will honor this document."

"What are we waiting for? Let's get going. I know it's in broad daylight, but it's my experience that people are less likely to call the police on people trying to get into a home in broad daylight as opposed to going in the dead of night."

SO CHRISTIAN and I headed to Max's house. We got there and Christian detected on his phone a security system. He was able to do his thing and disable it, and then he jimmied the lock. The two of us were in Max's house in no time.

The first thing I noticed about the house was that it looked like somebody was living there. There wasn't a mound of dust. I flipped on the lights. The fact the lights came on told me everything I needed to know. That meant Paul never turned off the utilities, which only confirmed my suspicions.

The house was cozy. The living room was smallish, with hardwood floors, a fireplace, several potted plants that looked well tended to, and a matching leather love seat and sofa. I smiled as I saw a new large-screen television right above the fireplace. That told me that not only was somebody staying there, but that person, who was no doubt Paul, bothered to outfit the place in new technology.

We went to the back bedroom. On the desk were three laptops, all of which looked brand-new. I nodded. My thought process was that Max owned his home, therefore he technically owned everything in it. No doubt Paul himself bought these computers, probably paying cash for them, and these were the computers where he downloaded his kiddie porn.

It was an ingenious plan, really. The IP address would be pinging from Max's home, Max's Internet account was being used to access this porn, and if the FBI ever decided to raid, there'd be plausible deniability all day long for Paul.

Paul could simply say he had no idea what they were talking about, this was his brother's home, he didn't go in there, and he had no idea where the computers came from.

Of course, the entire argument would break down with a simple DNA analysis of the computer and the home. And that was what I was planning to do with the computer. I would prove he was using it, and then I was going to use that against him.

I grabbed a hold of all of the computers in this home and took a look at the business card I had in my hand. Nathan Beaufort did private forensic analyses on computers, and he also had access to a lab that could do a DNA analysis of anything given to him.

I took the computers and then Christian and I went to dinner at the Shanghai Saloon. Over dumplings and Chinese beer, the two of us laughed at our caper. "Here's to making me a criminal," Christian said with a smile as he raised his glass of beer. "Next thing you know, you're going to have me burglarizing a home."

What we did wasn't really burglarizing, because we didn't commit a felony once we got on the premises. It wasn't even trespassing, because I had permission. But even I had to admit that what we did was a little bit shady.

Not that either of us would ever tell.

Chapter Nine

REGINA

REGINA WAS BECOMING MORE comfortable with her role, in spite of herself. She was slowly starting to get to know more and more of the girls, and she was beginning to understand what they were about and what made them tick.

She started with Britney. The two of them were sitting in the sunroom of the guesthouse where Britney and 19 of the other girls slept, dormitory style. There were four bedrooms in this guesthouse, and these bedrooms were enormous. Each bedroom had two bunk beds and one queen-sized bed. The girls took turns sleeping in the bunk beds and the one queen-sized bed. The house also had one common room, which had a large-screen TV, and several couches and loveseats. The common room had a large stone wall, with a fireplace and a big-screen TV, and the floor was hardwood cherry. While the bedrooms tended to be very messy, with clothes strewn around – after all, each room had five teenagers living there, so it was bound to be chaotic - the common room was always neat as a pin. There was a maid that came in every single day and cleaned up the common room, the kitchen, and the three bathrooms.

On any given day, there were usually five girls sitting around in the common room, watching reality TV while they all sat around and gossiped and chatted. They were teenagers, so most of them could still eat what they wanted and stay slim, and they did. They would eat pizzas, Chinese food ordered from Uber Eats, or burgers from In 'n' Out brought in by Door Dash. The reason why there were only five girls at a time hanging out in the common room eating junk food was because the other girls were out working, as the girls worked in shifts.

In addition to the common area, there was also a sunroom. This was a very small room that just had a couple of leather chairs. And Regina was starting to understand that Britney preferred to be alone in the sunroom. While the other girls were sitting and getting loud and dancing around the room to music videos, or having play fights, Britney was sitting quietly reading in the sunroom.

Regina knew that Britney would be ripe for her idea.

One day, about five weeks after Regina came to work for Carl, she found Britney in the sunroom.

"Hey, kid. What's going on?"

Britney just shrugged and said nothing.

"How come you're not out there with the other girls?" Regina asked her.

"I don't know. Those other girls get on my nerves. I mean, Morgan's okay, so is Brianna and Aisha. But the rest of the girls, I don't know. Sometimes I think I really don't belong here." She blinked.

Britney, like every other girl in the house, was a stunningly beautiful child. She had chestnut hair with auburn streaks, long dark eyelashes, blue eyes that were slightly almond-shaped, cheekbones that could cut glass, full lips and a long and graceful neck. She was one girl who Regina could see was being broken down by the experience. Regina knew that some of the girls were more affected by what was happening than other ones were. She didn't know if all of them knew how badly they were being exploited, but she felt Britney was acutely aware of it.

Regina opened her mouth. She'd worked on gaining Britney's trust, and, likewise, she was starting to feel she could trust Britney as well.

"Britney. If you and I had a little talk, do you promise not to tell anybody about what I'm saying to you?"

Britney nodded, and Regina shut the French doors that led from the sunroom to the common room. The sounds of shrieking girls in the common room were immediately silenced when Regina shut those doors.

Britney looked at the closed doors, then looked at Regina, and Regina could see both fear and curiosity in those eyes.

"Don't be afraid. I need to talk to you about what you just said, that you didn't feel you belonged here. Right?"

Britney nodded again. "Yes. I did say that. I don't feel like I belong here. I feel like I was meant to do something more than this. I don't really know what. I know I'm making good money here. And I don't know how I'd live outside of here. I mean, you and Jacqueline take such good care of me and everybody else. But I don't like what I'm doing with those men. I don't like it at all. It makes me sick. That's why I've not been working lately. I told Carl I needed some time off, and he let me have a few weeks of not working."

Britney was breathing heavily, and Regina knew she was on the verge of breaking down in tears.

Regina put her hand in Britney's thick dark hair. "Let me tell you about what I was doing when I was your age. My old man, he died. Shot dead by the side of the road by a guy high on PCP and on a countrywide crime spree. After that, my mom, she didn't want me. She took me from one place to another, one man to another. One of her guys, he raped me. So I split and lived on the streets, and I met a guy named Michael. He took me in, put me to work on the streets. I prostituted for him, he got me a job at a strip club too, and all the time I was doing that, I wasn't really doing it. I was checked out. You know, I'd never look a guy in the eye. I'd always look at the ceiling. I used to count the bumps on a popcorn ceiling while these men were doing whatever they were doing with me. I knew what I was doing was wrong, but I didn't know any other way of living, you know? I didn't know any other way of living."

Britney's eyes were getting wider and wider as Regina told her story. "What did you do?"

"I ended up in prison. Finally popped Michael. He was beating on me. I got out of prison because I found a lawyer who was able to show the jury I had reason to pop the guy. Now I'm out. And, again, what I say to you here cannot go out of this room, but I've made it a mission to help people being exploited. I'd like to help you."

"What do you mean? How can you help me?" She shook her head. "I'm only 14. I can't go back to my home, and I don't want to go into the system. I heard too many bad stories about kids who go into the system and get locked in closets and not fed by their foster families. Here I have friends and a beautiful room and all the food I want to eat. I can't leave this place."

"Oh, but you can. Trust me, you can."

She looked doubtful. "If I don't work here, I won't have

money. I can't live on my own. I'd have to go into the system, and the social work people, they'll have to contact my parents. That can't happen. My father was doing bad things to me. He was both raping me and beating on me. He's denied it. Every time somebody has investigated him, he denies it, and they believe him. He's a federal judge, Southern District of New York. Nobody will ever do anything to him. If I can't make money to support myself, I'll have to go into the system, and then I'll be right back with my dad."

Britney was shaking like a leaf, and Regina's heart went out to her. Regina was right where she was at one time. Couldn't stay at her home, couldn't live on her own, had to do what she had to to survive. Regina actually preferred prison to the life she had with her mother, after her father died, and to the life she had with Michael, prostituting herself and getting regularly beaten both by Michael and her johns. Her life was filled with such darkness and despair for so many years that she never imagined a way out. She found a way out, thank God, thanks to Avery, but if Avery didn't give her a chance, who would've?

So she knew what Britney was thinking and feeling. She got it. She was just going to have to convince Britney to take a chance that life could be better on the outside. She had to ask for Britney's trust that she could show her a way out.

"Britney, here's the thing. What Carl's doing to you is wrong. He's exploiting you and you can file a lawsuit against him. You and all the girls can sue him in a court of law and can get a lot of money out of him."

Britney's eyes got wider and wider as Regina talked to her about what she wanted to do. "I could get a lot of money out of him?" she asked. "But I'm hiding here. I'm hiding from law enforcement and my parents and anybody who might try to make me go back to my home. I'm safe here from them. If I get involved in a lawsuit, I won't be, will I?"

"You're a minor," Regina said. "The media won't expose you, if that's what you're worried about."

"No, that's not what I'm worried about," Britney said. "But, now that you mention it, I'd be afraid this whole thing would get out into the papers. I'm worried that if I did something like that, Carl would call my parents and tell them where I am. He told me that he'd always protect me from them. If I leave, they're going to find out where I am. They can't find me." She took a deep breath. "They just can't find me."

Regina suddenly understood that what she wanted to do would be more difficult than she'd anticipated. Britney was a trial balloon. She seemed to be the most vulnerable of all the girls, and possibly the person who might lead the way towards an exodus and a series of lawsuits that could bring this whole thing down.

At this point, she had to only hope that Britney wouldn't tell anybody about what Regina was asking of her. If she did, that could cause a lot of problems. She'd be gone and wouldn't be able to talk to any of the other girls. She would have failed. That was why she had to proceed gingerly with talking to vulnerable girls, because if she talked to any one of them, and that girl let it slip to the others, the whole plan would come tumbling down.

She would have to figure out a way to address Britney's concern for her own safety. Britney was right, unfortunately. Carl would go to her parents and send her back to them, and, since nobody believed her about her abuse allegations against her father, because her father was a powerful judge, they wouldn't believe her now, either. Not only that, but

Regina had to admit that if it came down to the girls filing a lawsuit against Carl, they all would be in danger. Carl would stop them by any means possible. He'd already shown that he possibly could get away with murder. These girls were all off the grid, aside from some of the ones sent here by their parents, so Carl could get away with killing most of them.

Carl probably wouldn't do the dirty work, but he certainly could give the deed to the Ivanov family. They were ruthless. Murdering is what they did with impunity. That was why Carl was partnering with them. They were his enforcer. They kept everybody in line.

She would have to try something else to get to where she wanted to go.

All she needed was one girl. Just one. But she felt like she tried with Britney, and she had to be much more circumspect.

"Listen, Britney, please don't tell anybody about our talk. Okay?"

She nodded and said nothing.

Regina got up and went into the common room, where there were four girls laying around on various couches and bean bags. Some series was showing on Netflix, and about half the girls were watching it, and half were doing other things. One girl was braiding another girl's hair. Another was giving a pedicure to one of the girls. Several of them were eating pizza and gabbing.

Regina went out to the pool area, where several girls were swimming. There already were several men out there with them. One old guy had his arm around a young girl's back while they both hung onto the side of the pool. Another old guy was sitting on a lounge chair, chatting with a couple of girls sitting together on a different lounge chair.

Regina worried that she blew it. Girls talked too much.

They tended to gossip about whatever was going on in their lives, and she knew that the other girls were going to ask Britney about what they were talking about behind closed doors for all that time.

She would have to approach the entire thing in a different way.

Just then, she had an idea.

She went to Carl and explained that she had to leave for the afternoon. He let her go, asking her to be back for the evening's events, and she got into her car.

She would head to the courthouse to find some records. And then head to the penitentiary. Her idea was a Hail Mary of sorts, but, at this point, she would have to take what she could get.

Chapter Ten

AVERY

June 1998

BECKY TOLD me about what she was doing with Carl Williams, and I became afraid for her. It didn't sound kosher to me, not at all.

But there was something bothering me even more than her apparent obsession with a much older man. I realized there was a good possibility she had a drug problem.

The thing of it was, Becky was very open with me about the things she was up to when I wasn't around. And it wasn't just the fact that she had kids from her school come over, when her parents were not there, and I knew they smoked marijuana. I also knew more than a few of them snorted cocaine in the home. I tried to look the other way about that. I didn't really care about the marijuana. As far as I was concerned, it was no worse than alcohol. And I knew lots of kids in my high school, let alone in Becky's upscale private school, were into smoking marijuana. Big deal. Kids will do what kids will do.

But the cocaine thing, that was something else entirely. I was vaguely aware that cocaine can kill you the first time you try it. That made me afraid to ever try it.

"Listen, you're such a square. My dad does it. I know he does it. I came home one night after a party. He was sitting in the living room and had some lines right out in front of him. Right there on the coffee table. And he was wasted. He had to have been extremely wasted, because he saw me coming in the door and didn't even try to put it away. I mean, I'm surprised he didn't invite me to try it with him. I really was hoping he would."

I had a hard time believing any father would do that. But then again, maybe I shouldn't have had a hard time believing it. Pete Whitfield was the type of dad who had no problem giving his daughter a gin and tonic while she lay in the pool. And he apparently was the type a guy who had no problem giving his daughter cocaine when she wanted it.

"What about your mom, what does she say about your father getting high like that?"

Becky just shrugged. "I don't know. She's too busy with her boyfriend. Yes, she has a boy toy on the side. I've met him. When my dad goes out of town, she brings this guy around. He's some dude by the name of Antonio something. My dad knows all about that guy, too. And I don't think he cares my mom is getting strange because he gets strange too. Come on, don't you know this is how the other half lives? Are you not aware of this fact?"

I felt incredibly naïve. We were only 15 years old. This should've been a time of first dates, first kisses, studying hard in school so we could get into the best college. I felt sad that Becky was growing up long before she should have been. She had terrible role models in her parents. And I knew she would think that all of this was normal. It was normal for people to be married yet having affairs. It was normal to be wasted on drugs right in front of your kids.

But it wasn't normal. It should never be considered normal.

Just then, while Becky told me about a party she was going to go to at a friend's house, where there would be hard drugs shared by all, she got up to answer her cell phone. She looked at the screen and rolled her eyes.

"I'm sorry, but I have to take this. I keep telling this guy to leave me the hell alone, but he won't take the hint. But I'm gonna have to tell him again."

She shut her door and I could hear her talking loudly on the other side. "I told you never to call me again. I tried to explain to you that I don't want to see you anymore. I don't know why you can't get this through your head."

There was a pause on the other end of the line, and then Becky started to talk loudly. "I know, I know. I know you're my supplier. But you have to know that I can find other people to supply me with what I need as well. I don't need you. I don't need you at all. Quite frankly, you creep me out. Now are you gonna stop calling me or what?"

I could almost see Becky rolling her eyes while she spoke on the phone with this guy, whoever he was. "Oh? I guess that's my answer then, right? You won't stop calling me. Well maybe I should tell your dad about what you're doing here. I don't think he'd be very happy about it."

Another long pause and then Becky started talking even louder. "Listen, you cock-sucker, when I tell you you need to leave me alone, I mean it. Don't force me to change my number."

And then Becky apparently hung up on him. At least I deduced that much because she was no longer speaking and then she came out of the room. "I'm sorry. Listen, I have to get going. I'm supposed to see Carl tonight. He's having a party and I'm supposed to be one of the guests of honor."

I wanted to go to the party with her. I wanted to see what was going on. "Hey, maybe I could come with you?"

She shook her head. "No. It's not your scene. Trust me on this. Well, you have fun tonight doing whatever you're doing. I'll probably see you Monday. Carl wants me to stay the whole weekend."

The next thing I knew, Becky was getting ready to go to some party. She dressed really sexy for this party. Tiny little dress that showed off all of her assets and high heels. Her strawberry hair was piled up on her head, and she put on so much makeup it looked like you couldn't take it off with a chisel. One thing was for sure, she looked a lot older than what she was.

I just had a sinking feeling Becky was heading for disaster.

Chapter Eleven

AVERY

Present Day

I FELT sick when I got the results back from the computers I sent in for forensic analysis. While Nathan found the computers that Christian and I took from Max's house had child porn on them, he also found there wasn't any kind of DNA or fingerprints he could get off it.

"Looks like it's been cleaned pretty well," he said.

Of course it was cleaned well I thought. Paul wasn't as stupid as I thought. Without his DNA, how could I prove he was the one accessing the child porn?

I went down to Christian's office. "We're going to have to go to Plan B," I said.

Christian nodded his head. "Let's do it," he said.

Christian and I had talked about setting up surveillance equipment remotely. The only thing we needed was to go to Max and get his permission to set this up. Max had a legitimate purpose for having surveillance for his house. It was vacant, after all. Then, if Christian could set it up, I could catch Paul in the act of downloading the porn. At any rate, I could prove he was the one using the computers in that room.

But first, it was imperative that Christian and I got back into that house and put those computers back. We also had to hope a nosy neighbor didn't already talk to Paul and tell him about Christian and I getting into this home and taking the computers out. If that happened, the entire plan would fall apart. Paul would be put on notice that something was going on and he wouldn't go back to what he was doing if that were the case.

I needed Paul to keep doing what he was doing. I needed to get that kind of leverage over him, so he not only would bring charges against Carl but also see to it those charges stuck. If he went to trial against Carl, he wouldn't be playing hide the ball like he was with my case.

Christian and I made the trip out to Bakersfield to see Max.

We went through the procedures to visit Max in the common visiting room, and then Christian and I sat at one of the tables and waited for him to come out. He appeared in about 20 minutes.

"Hey," he said to me, with a smile. "What happened? Did you go over to my house?"

"We did and we took some of computers we found in one of the bedrooms. There were three different computers in there, all of them brand-new. And one of them had thousands of images of child pornography on it. Unfortunately, I tried to get a DNA or fingerprint analysis done on the computer, and it turns out the guy knows how to wipe his computer clean. So I feel we have to have overwhelming evidence that the guy is the one downloading the kiddy porn before I can convince a prosecutor to bring charges against him. That's where you come in."

Max was nodding along as I spoke. "So, my brother's a perv." He shook his head. "Figures."

"What do you mean?"

"Listen, Paul hasn't had the easiest life. He was molested by a priest when he was very young. He's gone through counseling and all that, but we were warned he might act out like this. And, well, I guess he is. Acting out, that is. His mind is completely warped because of what happened to him. Anyhow, I'm sorry he's doing this."

I felt a twinge of sympathy for Paul. In a way, he was like many of my clients. The guilty clients usually had a terrible story to tell about what made them that way. They would tell me about fetal alcohol syndrome, abuse, neglect, head injuries, any number of things, and that always made me want to go to the mattresses for them in court. No matter what they did.

But I would have to set it all aside for Paul. I had to remember that Paul was dirty enough to send me to prison for the rest of my life, knowing I did nothing wrong. I had to not forget that fact.

"I'm very sorry to hear about your brother," I said to Max. "Listen, here's what Christian and I want to do. We want to put surveillance in your home. We want to catch Paul in the act of downloading porn or accessing it from the computer. Only then will I have enough evidence to have leverage over him or, even better, have enough evidence to bring to a prosecutor and have him put away. Where he belongs. He's not just accessing child porn, he's actually living out his fantasies as well. He's a part of an elite pedophilia ring in Del Mar."

Just then, it hit me. I wondered how Paul had the money

for the dues for Carl's ring. I remembered that Carl talked about how the dues were $50,000 per month. I just figured Carl might've given Paul a free pass because Paul allowed him to go free for Becky's murder. To me, that was damning evidence that Carl actually was the person who killed Becky. It would've been quid pro quo - "I'll cover up evidence for you and make sure somebody else pays for murdering Becky, in exchange for your giving me a lifetime membership to your exclusive club."

But what if that wasn't the case? What if Paul actually had the money for that exclusive club? Would that make the evidence against Carl weaker?

"You said Paul was molested by a priest," I said. "Did he actually get money for that? Did he sue?"

"Yeah," Max said. "He sued. Got $20 million for it. Why do you ask?"

I just shook my head. "No reason." He got $20 million because he was molested by a priest. Did that mean anything? Was that a fact I could use?

One thing was for sure, though. Even though the dues for Carl's ring came out to $600,000 per year, Paul definitely had the money to pay. So it was possible his membership in that club wasn't a freebie.

I handed Max a document that gave me permission to set up his house with surveillance equipment. We went and found a notary, Max signed the document, and then Christian and I were on our way.

———

ONCE I GOT into my car, I looked over at Christian. "So we found out Paul is actually a rich man. What does that mean?"

"It means there's one more person we can bring into this lawsuit," Christian said. "Why?"

"I don't know. I just wonder if it's significant somehow, that's all. I mean, the fact that he's independently wealthy kinda shoots holes into one theory I had as to how Paul affords membership at Carl's club. But it also shoots holes into another theory I had."

"What's that?"

"Well, it seems he probably wasn't bribeable. I mean, Regina checked his financials and didn't find any money changing hands from Carl to Paul back in the day. But I always there had to have been a different bank account somewhere where those transfers would've shown up."

"There obviously was a different bank account," Christian said. "I mean, there's obviously an account that has all those millions of dollars in it. I found evidence of some of his accounts online when I hacked, but I must've missed a major account. It probably isn't on-line. It's probably an account set up under a dummy account or perhaps was set up with a shell LLC. We're going to have to figure that one out. Maybe that's the account that showed money changed hands."

"So there still might be evidence of bribery from Carl to Paul but we just haven't found it yet, then."

"Right. But what else are you thinking about?"

"I don't know. I just wonder if we're barking up the wrong tree here with Carl. I mean, he's a bad guy. A very bad guy. I'm burning with the desire to bring him down, just because what he's doing with those girls is very, very wrong. It's devastating for them. It's going to mess them up for the rest of their lives. But I don't know. Something's off. I just wonder if Carl was behind Becky's murder in the first place. I mean, it could be that Paul joined Carl's club not because Paul covered up Carl's murder, but because Paul has the cash to join. Nothing more than that."

As I spoke aloud, I realized I had a nagging feeling, all along, that Carl might not have done Becky's murder. Now the nagging feeling just became that much more acute. The small voice inside of me was getting louder and louder. As much as I wanted to quiet it, I just couldn't.

"So you think Paul might've been covering up for somebody else, then? Where are you going with this, Avery?" Christian asked.

"I don't know. Paul was definitely covering for somebody. Why he was covering for this person, I don't really know. At any rate, I still want to bring him down. He's still responsible for my imprisonment. So I still want to go with our original plans. And then, well, I'm going to have to figure out which direction I want to go with it. Either use it as leverage so Paul will agree to bring down a bigger fish, like Carl, or just go straight to the FBI and show them my evidence of what he's doing. If he goes to prison for being into child porn, and being into pedophilia, I won't shed a tear. That's just one less creep in the world."

I heard Christian sigh and I knew him well enough by now to understand that when he sighed like that, he was holding his tongue about something.

"What?" I demanded. "What's wrong with those plans?"

"Listen, Avery, I agree we should do this for leverage. But, come on, you're a criminal defense attorney. You defend people who do really crappy things and you do it for a living. Yet you're talking about this guy like he's the absolute scum of the earth. And why? Because he was responsible for you going to prison. That's the only reason why. I just think you need to be honest with yourself. If this guy wasn't responsible for your prison sentence, you probably would be taking him on as a client as opposed to being hell-bent on bringing him down."

I took a deep breath. I didn't want to react in anger to the horrible things Christian was saying. I wanted to process and analyze them. I needed to dig deep and try to figure out if there was any truth to what he was saying.

It was true that I defended people like Paul. People who were child molesters and into child porn. Usually, they were one and the same. Not that I ever tried a case with a person guilty of pedophilia or possession of child porn. I'd never actually try to get an acquittal for a guilty person. But I did work with the prosecutors to try to get as light of a sentence as possible.

Yet, here I was, trying to burn Paul at the stake. Was I a hypocrite?

"Avery? You there? Or did you check out after my calling you out like that? I mean, I'm sorry. I really am. I just want you to be a bit more intellectually honest on why you're doing this. I agree this is important. You can probably get this guy to spill the beans on who he was covering for when he railroaded you into prison. I think that's the most important thing here. Yes, if we don't turn him into the FBI, he's going to keep doing what he's doing. I understand that. But if we turn him into the FBI, we won't get the chance to ask him the questions we need to ask him. And that means the bigger fish will get away. You have to look at the big picture here, Avery. Stay focused on that."

I nodded and focused on my white knuckles which were gripping the steering wheel of my SUV. "I know. The person who killed Becky was a child murderer. That person needs to be brought down. And Paul can help us do that. Big picture. Big picture."

"Don't let the perfect be the enemy of the good," Christian said. "We do this right and your false imprisonment is avenged and a child murderer is off the street. We jump the gun and Paul might end up behind bars, which is a fine outcome, but the child murderer will slip through our fingers. I don't know about you, but I don't want that to happen."

———

WE GOT to Max's home, and, just like last time, Christian disabled the security system and the two of us jimmied the lock on the front door. I made a beeline for the bedroom, and, to my relief, the computers were still in the same position as before. I was afraid Paul might've become wise to what we were doing and hid the computers away. Or maybe destroyed them. But that wasn't the case.

Christian busied himself with hiding a microscopic camera in the wall. Nobody could detect it unless you were specifically looking for it, and, even then, it would've been almost impossible to find without some kind of high-tech equipment. It wasn't something silly like planting a teddy bear with a camera in it, which was what parents did all the time to watch their nannies in action. No, this was much more sophisticated than that. Christian had access to the latest in technology, and, for that, I was grateful.

It took him the better part of an hour, and then, when he was done, he slapped his hands together. "Okay, it's in position. This little camera can pan all the way around the room, so, even if he decides to switch positions, the camera will still pick it up."

"What about putting one in the living room? Or in the other bedroom?"

"Good thinking," he said. And then he spent the next two hours putting cameras in the other rooms.

He got through with all this and the two of us slinked out of the house. It was dark by that time, which was a good thing. I was still paranoid a nosy neighbor would tip him off on what was going on. But I never saw anybody around when Christian and I were doing our thing, so I had to hope and pray nobody saw us. It seemed like this was a neighborhood where people weren't around during the day, so we were probably safe.

———

TWO DAYS LATER, I got my answer. Christian had been monitoring the feed at Max's house, and one night, he texted me. "Get online and look at this," he said, giving me the site that he was accessing, his username and password.

I logged in, and my heart was pounding as I wondered what I would see when I logged on.

And there it was.

Paul was sitting in front of his computer. I could see the images on the computer, and they were clearly that of a pre-pubescent girl and boy. They were both nude and touching each other. While Paul watched it, he was clearly masturbating.

We had him.

Now what?

Chapter Twelve

REGINA

REGINA FOUND out as much information as she could about Emma's father. She'd gotten to know Emma, who was the 14-year-old with the millionaire father nailed for embezzlement. The mother had sent Emma into prostitution because she didn't want to lose her big fancy house in La Jolla.

Regina had no use for the mother. She was too far gone, as far as Regina was concerned. There wasn't a thing she could use from a woman like that. But the father, now that was another story. Regina would go into this dude's background and see what he did. Better yet, if he was a millionaire, he probably had some connections of his own.

Regina started with the court records for the guy. His name was Harrison Baker. As Emma said, he was apparently a very wealthy person. At least he was at one time. Emma was wrong, however, as to why the guy ended up in prison. It wasn't that he was embezzling from his company. From what Regina could read, the guy went down for racketeering. She read further, and found out he was involved in running for the Aslanian clan. The Aslanian clan were Armenian mobsters who ran the territory from Los Angeles down to Oceanside, and what Harrison was doing for them was hacking. He was involved in identity theft and was responsible for obtaining the social security numbers of thousands of people in one incident, and, in another incident, was the mastermind behind breaching a major credit agency and obtaining sensitive information for millions of this agency's customers.

For this, he was apparently paid very good money. He'd been doing it for a period of twenty years, and, during this period of time, was paid millions. According to the statement of information for the guy, he was finally brought down by the FBI after he breached the Department of Defense. He obtained some some top-secret classified information about an assassination plot carried out by the CIA. It was a foiled plot, because he got that information and threatened to blow the whistle by giving that information to a reporter with the New York *Times*. He told the cops that he wanted this information for his clan, because they demanded it from him. The person who was to be assassinated was an Armenian diplomat, and the assassination was to take place in New York City. On U.S. soil, in other words.

This was fascinating reading for Regina. More than that, it presented her a roadmap on how to use this guy. Yeah, Carl had some high-level prosecutors, judges and cops in his pocket. He used those contacts to stay "above the law." But what if Regina nabbed somebody even more powerful than those people? This guy was put into prison before he could reveal the details about this CIA assassination plot. Regina wondered what else he knew. She wondered what kind of dirt he had on other people. She also wondered if he'd be willing to use any kind of information he had to make sure that somebody made Carl pay for what he was doing.

She had to take that chance. So she went to the prison with the intention of talking to him. Once she told him what his daughter was doing, she hoped he'd be angry enough to marshal forces on the outside to do something. She knew something about the Aslanian clan, and, as far as she knew, it was more powerful than the Ivanovs, but they apparently worked with the Ivanovs, among other Eastern European mob families.

———

WHEN SHE GOT to the prison to speak with Harrison, however, she was surprised to see a familiar face. It was the guy who'd been hanging around the pool at some of the parties, the guy who was always just observing everybody and not partaking in the festivities.

He was coming out of the prison as she was coming in, and the two of them exchanged glances.

He smiled. "Regina, right?" he asked, pointing to her.

"Yeah," she said, thinking it was really weird this guy was here. What was he doing here? "Right."

"Hey, I've been seeing you around, and I've never gotten the chance to formally introduce myself. My name is Jackson Eisel."

"Yeah, I've been seeing you around, all right." Regina felt her hackles rising up. "I've been seeing you around those parties."

"Uh, huh. I had a feeling about you. Don't worry, I won't tell anybody you're some kind of mole. I mean, I won't tell anybody about that if you don't tell anybody I'm also a mole. I mean, I'm right, aren't I? You got that job there because you wanted to infiltrate the place? I've been watching you and I just get the distinct vibe you aren't there to work. You're there to spy."

Regina didn't trust this guy any further than she could throw him. Carl might've tailed her and sent this guy to this prison because he wanted her to confess about what she was doing. No way would she tell this guy a thing. She knew that if Carl ever found out that she was, in fact, a mole, she wouldn't live to see her next birthday, which was in two weeks.

"Yeah, you got me all wrong, there. I'm there for one reason, and one reason only. I'm there for Carl. I'm there to fluff old guys and for moral support for the girls. Now, if you'll excuse me…"

"And why are you here, then?" Jackson asked her. "What brings you to this place? Do you have somebody in here you're seeing? Maybe somebody you need to ask certain questions of?" He raised an eyebrow.

"I might ask you the same thing," she said. "Why are you here?"

"I'm not going to answer that question," he said. "You won't come clean with me, so I won't say anything more to you about why I'm here. But if you ever want to come clean on what you're really all about, here's my card."

He handed her a business card. It simply had his name and phone number on it. No other information.

"What's this? This has no information on it."

"It has all the information you need. Trust me, I'm one of the good guys. You don't have to take my word for it but I hope maybe you will." At that, he smiled broadly at Regina and then proceeded to walk out of the lobby of the prison registration building. "I hope you find what you're looking for. But if you ever need an ally, you just give me a call. I was thinking maybe you and I could team up."

At that, he walked out the door. Regina stared at the business card in her hand, as the woman behind the bullet-proof glass waited for her to give the name of the person she was going to see.

"I'm here to see Harrison Baker," Regina said.

"You on his visiting list?" the woman asked her.

"No. This is a professional visit." She showed the woman her private investigator credentials and the woman nodded and picked up the phone. "He can see you." Then she got out a map of the prison and all the pods, and then showed her which pod he was in. "Just go in there, tell the guard who you're there to see, and he'll direct you to the visiting area. Since you're a professional, you don't have to always be here during visiting hours, although it is helpful."

"Thanks," Regina said, looking at the map.

She found the pod that housed Harrison and found a guard who led her to the visiting room. There, she waited for Harrison to be brought out.

This prison wasn't a maximum security, but, rather, was a medium security penitentiary. This was generally the place where guys like Harrison, convicted for non-violent crimes, yet don't quite qualify for Club Fed, go. There was an electrified fence around the perimeter. There weren't rock concerts and pool halls, but, at the same time, the inmates did get certain privileges the Max prisoners didn't.

Harrison came out to see her about an hour after she arrived. He cocked his head and smiled at her. "Well, well, well, to what do I owe this pleasure?" he asked her. "Who sent you?"

"Calm down," Regina said. "I'm not here with a nail file in a cake. And I'm not here to give you some kind of conjugal visit. I'm here to ask you some questions. I'm also here to tell you about what your daughter is up to."

"My daughter? Emma?" Harrison squinted his eyes. "What is she doing? What is my baby girl doing?" All of a sudden, the happy-go-lucky guy Regina met when she first came into the prison turned into somebody completely different. She could see rage behind his eyes.

This might work after all. "Your daughter, Emma, was forced into prostitution by your loving wife, Jennifer. Jennifer apparently feels it's necessary to maintain your home in La Jolla, and, well, she doesn't actually want to go out and get a job to pay the mortgage on that fancy home, so she's making your daughter work for that $5,000 a month mortgage payment."

Regina folded her arms while she watched Harrison's face change from anger to down-and-dirty rage. She smiled, knowing she had calculated it all correctly.

This guy would help her.

Chapter Thirteen

AVERY

I DID IT. Well, actually, Christian did it. He managed to capture just the kind of incriminating evidence that would give us a ton of leverage over Paul the perv.

Now it was just a matter of Christian and I using this information against him. It helped that Paul was a longtime prosecutor. He first got into this office over 20 years ago, right after he moved out here from Kansas City. He had moved up the ranks and was currently running for the job of District Attorney. In other words, the guy had ambition. Of course, I knew there was little chance he would ever become district attorney, and, even if he did, it would only be a matter of time before somebody blackmailed him with his predilections. That kind of thing can't stay quiet forever. But for now, I was content with simply threatening him with what I knew.

I made an appointment to see him. The appointment was for the next day at 2 PM. That gave me time to get my ducks in a row before our visit. I was prepared with a thumb drive of what I had recorded at his house, and I knew exactly how to threaten him with this. In fact, I felt gleeful that I would finally get to watch this guy squirm like a worm on a hook. Just like he watched me squirm all those years ago, knowing I was innocent, hiding evidence from the court, watching me be taken away in handcuffs... there were no words for the fury I felt for this guy.

Chapter Fourteen

THE NEXT DAY, I met with him in his office. I just looked at his smug face, knowing he probably took some kind of sadistic pleasure about what he did to me all those years ago. I wanted to slap him. I instead just took a breath and looked him right in the eye.

"Avery Collins, to what do I owe this pleasure? I know we don't have any cases together."

That was the other thing. I had to work with this guy. He was a prosecutor on many of my criminal cases over the years. It always made me want to throw up in my mouth a little bit every time I saw he was my prosecutor, but I always had to smile and bear it.

"Actually, I wanted to speak with you about a case I want you to file. I want you to file a murder case against Carl Williams. I have a strong suspicion he was behind the murder of Becky Whitfield. You know, the case you railroaded me into? That case?"

At that, the bastard started to laugh. "Oh, really? And what, pray tell, evidence do you have against him?"

"He's the leader of an elite pedophilia ring up in Del Mar. The clientele pay $50,000 a month just to take part in this ring. I have reason to believe Becky was a part of this sick scene, and I have reason to believe that Carl killed her because she was going to expose him."

I actually didn't have reason to believe that Becky was going to expose him. That was just a hunch. All I really wanted Paul to do was file charges against Carl, and then he could come up with the evidence against him.

He shook his head. "No can do. Sorry. You're going to have to come up with a more substantial answer than that. Number one, how do you know he has a pedophilia ring? Number two, I investigated him all those years ago for that murder. He had an airtight alibi. He was at an international conference in Geneva at the time. I checked, he really was there. And I spoke with several witnesses at this conference, high-level diplomats and such, and they confirmed to me he really was there. So, I'm sorry, you're just gonna have to try again."

My heart sunk when he said that. "Listen, you were covering for somebody. I know that. Perhaps Carl wasn't the person behind it, but I have definitive proof he's the head of an elite pedophilia ring and I want to bring it down. I want you to bring charges against him for that."

Paul took a deep breath and steepled his hands. "Do you understand what you're asking me to do? Carl Williams is an extremely wealthy man. And he has ties in the community I don't want to mess with. So, I'm sorry, but I'm going to have to decline your demand. Now, is there anything else you want to ask me because I'm a very busy man?" He didn't look at me as he spoke.

I thought about what he was saying to me, about how Carl wasn't behind the murder of Becky. I would have to get

Regina to look into his alibi, but my heart sunk when I realized I might be back to square one on that situation.

Yet there was still something I could do about Carl's disgusting ring. And I was going to do it.

"You *will* file charges against Carl Williams, and you *will* be responsible for breaking up his pedophilia ring. If you don't, I'll expose you."

"Expose me for what?"

"Expose you for what you do at your brother Max's house."

I watched his face and saw all the color draining out of it. All at once, his hands were fidgeting. He got up out of his chair and started pacing around the room.

"I don't know what you're talking about," he said meekly, almost pathetically.

"Oh, but you do know what I'm talking about. I have proof. I've paid a couple of visits to your brother Max, and Max has been more than helpful. He's given me access to his house and he's allowed me to set up a surveillance system. I've also taken the computers I found in his house over to a forensic analysis computer guy, and this guy confirmed to me that one of the computers in the bedroom, Max's bedroom, is full of child porn. Do you need me to go on?"

He swallowed hard. I could see his Adam's apple bobbing up and down. "What are you going to do?"

"You know what I'm going to do. I'm going to take this thumb drive, which has all these images and videos of you enjoying yourself while you watched very young boys and girls on screen, and I'm going to send it to your immediate supervisor. I think he'll be very interested in it and I think he'll be eager to file charges against you. And if he doesn't, I'm going to the media about why the district attorney is not only keeping a pedophile on his payroll, but he's refusing to file charges against him. I'm going to make it a scandal like this city has never seen. That's what I plan to do with what's on this thumb drive."

He took a deep breath. And then his voice was pleading with me. "You don't understand. You don't understand. If I file charges against Carl, it'll be my life. Carl has friends who are not nice. To say the very least. If I file charges against him, I'll be dead by sundown."

"Don't be silly. You file charges against him, and then it's out there in the media and he wouldn't dare do anything to you. He has to know that if he sends one of his mob goons to bump you off, there will be hell to pay. That would be a clear RICO violation, and the feds would get involved. He's going to have to deal with the FBI if he has you killed, and I think he wouldn't want that headache. You just have to tell him the jig is up. It's either you prosecuting him or the feds. He's going to have to pick his poison, and if he has you killed, he's going to have one more thing to answer for. And, trust me, the FBI won't go easy on him."

"You're signing my death warrant."

"Cry me a river. You had no problem signing my death warrant. Or do you remember that? And while we're at it, I need to know exactly why you signed my death warrant all those years ago. Why you were so eager to allow me to go to prison for the rest of my life for something I didn't do. You were covering for somebody, I assumed it was for Carl, but it apparently wasn't. At least, if you're not lying about the fact that Carl had an airtight alibi for the time of Becky's death, and that somebody else was involved. I need to know who it was."

Paul didn't answer me. In fact, he just stared at me. "So this is what it comes down to. This is what my miserable life has come to. I tried so hard all these years to calm my demons. You don't know what it's like to deal with what I'm dealing with. Who I'm dealing with. If you did, you wouldn't be putting this on me. But that's okay. I know what I need to do. And I'm at peace with that. Now, I'd appreciate it if you would leave this office now."

I didn't budge. "I need your commitment. I need to hear from your mouth that you're going to file charges against Carl. He might not have been behind Becky's murder, I don't know, I'm going to have to look into that alibi situation myself, but, even if he wasn't, he is behind the destruction of hundreds of girls. You need to do something about that. Nobody else is willing to do anything about it, but I don't think you really have a choice in the matter."

He just shook his head.

And then, he picked up his chair and flung it hard against the window. Before I could react, he'd broken the window with his heavy black chair.

And then, with one leap, he threw himself out that window, onto the cement below.

Chapter Fifteen

REGINA

"YEAH, Harrison, your daughter is prostituting herself as part of the Carl Williams ring." Regina said to Harrison. "On the good side, your wife is entertaining random gentleman at your $1.5 million dollar La Jolla manse. Her lifestyle hasn't been affected at all by your incarceration. Your daughter is bringing in $10,000 a month, because she's working a lot of hours, and your wife is busy as well. She's busy getting mani-pedis, massages, facials in more ways than one, and she's planning on sailing around the world with one of her new boyfriends. I don't know if you feel good about what's going on but I certainly don't."

"That bitch. Listen, you get my daughter out of there, you hear that? You get her out of there."

"Here's the thing. Your daughter is just one of many young girls living over there. I mean, she's a day player, which means she actually lives with your wife, that is when your wife happens to be home, which is not often. But there's lots of girls over there. I could certainly get your daughter out of there, not that she would go, because she's making too much money, because she doesn't understand she's being exploited. But I want this ring to come down and I want these girls to be compensated for what they went through. They're all going to be messed up for the rest of their lives, they're all going to need lots and lots of therapy, and I want them to be compensated. That's where you come in. I need a little bit of insurance that if those girls actually leave the compound, nobody will end up dead. And that would include me."

Regina could see Harrison getting the picture. "There are some people who owe me some favors," he said. "I took the fall for a guy by the name of Alexander Petrov. He's a brigadier in the Ivanov clan. The Ivanovs are close allies of the Aslanians. I agreed to take the fall for him because, basically, he's too important to the organization. The Ivanovs made sure I wasn't put into a maximum-security prison, and they made sure my prison time was short. I only got five years for what I was convicted of, which was the murder of a high-level government guy trying to expose our organization. Actually, I wasn't convicted for that, even though that was what I was charged with. I was only convicted for the hacking offense for when I got into the Department of Defense to find out information about what that guy was doing. I didn't really kill that guy. Alexander did. Anyhow, nobody's going to pay the price for murdering that guy, because I agreed to take the sentence for Alexander."

"You do know that the Ivanovs are behind the whole Carl Williams thing?" Regina asked. "They're the enforcers. They make sure nothing ever happens to Carl. If we could neutralize them, I could get the girls out of there safely, and then I can turn the tables on Carl to make sure the girls are compensated for all the crap they're going through right now. They can never be made whole, but they can get out, and they can have money once they get out. Probably a lot of money if my boss Avery does things right."

"All right, all right, I'm thinking here," Harrison said. "Listen, I may get a message to a guy I know by the name of Mikhail Vasiliev. Mikhail is also a brigadier in the Ivanov clan, but he's higher up than Alexander. He's right under Yuri Ivanov. I think I'm going to have to have a word with him. I'm going to tell him he needs to tell Yuri to drop Carl as a partner. I have enough dirt on the entire Ivanov clan that if I really wanted to, I could start cooperating fully with the FBI. They're already offering me protection in exchange for my giving testimony about what happened to that government official and everything else I've been involved with over the years. I'm going to tell Alexander I'll take that deal unless he tells Yuri to drop Carl."

"Will that work?" Regina asked excitedly.

"Of course it'll work. Listen, Yuri has business alliances everywhere. He cuts ties with people all the time. He's pretty cold-blooded when it comes to the people he cuts ties with, even if they're making a lot of money, as I'm sure this ring probably is. All I need to do is give the word I'm about to sing. I'm protected heavily back here, so they can't get to me. I give that word, and, within a few days, you'll find Yuri is no longer partnering with Carl. That'll leave Carl vulnerable. I still don't think he'll be prosecuted for what he's doing because he has too much crap on everybody in town. But without the Ivanov family to back him up, I think you could get the girls out of there safely."

Would it really be as easy as that? This guy just gives the word and Carl no longer has an enforcer on his side?

Could she trust Harrison? The better question was, what choice did she have? This guy was literally the only game in town as far as she was concerned. She had to put her faith in him because that was the only way her and Avery's plan could work.

"Thank you for doing this."

"No. I need to thank you for coming to tell me about what my daughter is doing. And I need to thank you for getting her out of there. I'll do anything for her. And if you ever see my wife, you tell her I'm coming for her when I get out. I don't play that shit."

At that, he got up from the table and shook Regina's hand. "You just sit tight. You give me a couple of days and I can guarantee you the Ivanov family won't play a factor in the Carl Williams sicko ring. And then you can be free to take the girls out of there and do whatever you need to do."

Regina smiled as she got up and left the pod and made the long walk to her car in the parking lot of the prison. While she wouldn't count her chickens before they hatched, she felt confident something would happen. At least the first step would happen. She would get the girls out of there and Avery would file a lawsuit on their behalf.

For the first time since the entire mess got started, Regina actually felt hopeful.

Chapter Sixteen

AVERY

I STOOD there in shock until I opened the door to Paul's office. There were people milling about and I went up to the receptionist desk. "Um, I have to report, um, an accident."

It was then that the police arrived in the office. After Paul's body hit the pavement below, there was a lot of pandemonium and the cops were called immediately. Paul was evidently identified by his prosecutor's badge in his wallet, which led the cops straight to the District Attorney's Office.

Since I was a witness to what happened, I had to go down to the police station and give them my statement. I was shaking and in shock, and there was a part of me that was feeling extremely selfish about the entire situation. Now that Paul was dead, what? What would happen? How could I ever find out who exactly killed Becky all those years ago? I kicked myself mentally. I should not have been so aggressive with him. I should've simply told him what I had and left it at that. Did I really have to tell him in such explicit detail exactly how things would go? Could I not foresee that he would be backed into a corner so he knew it was either he be murdered by a member of the Ivanov clan or be exposed for the entire world to see? I gave him absolutely no way out. Well, that wasn't right. I did give him a way out, and that way out was straight to the pavement of Third and Broadway.

———

I GOT down to the police station and answered questions for the next two hours. However, I didn't tell them what I did to precipitate him jumping out that window. If I told them that, I would be guilty of criminal extortion at the very least. If they were going to be really creative about it, they could probably charge me with Paul's murder. There was no way I would risk that so I lied to the cops. I told them I didn't know why Paul would've jumped out the window. Perhaps he had some kind of deep-seated guilt about what he did to me all those years ago and he couldn't live with himself, so when he saw me in his office, it just tripped him.

The cops seemed satisfied with what I told him.

"Well, Ms. Collins, your story about him prosecuting your case checked out. I just had an assistant do some research on what you were telling me about how he was responsible for you being falsely imprisoned and she produced this newspaper article for me. It talks about how you were let out of prison and how the prosecutor in the case had apparently concealed evidence. I'm going to take you at your word that that might've been the reason why he jumped out of the window while you were in his office. This is not the end of the investigation, I hope you understand. I'm going to have to speak with some other witnesses. But, for now, you're free to go."

As I left the police station, I felt the heavy burden of what I just did. I just lied to the cops. I was responsible for a man's death. Granted, it was the man responsible for my imprisonment, but that didn't make make me feel any better about his fate. And there was a part of me that was terrified the cops would find out the truth about what really transpired in that office - they would find out I was extorting Paul at the time he jumped out that window. I would always have to be looking over my shoulder, afraid the cops would come to my door anytime and arrest me for making criminal threats.

Maybe even arrest me for his murder.

Chapter Seventeen

WHEN I GOT in the car, I turned on my phone and saw Regina had called me several times.

I immediately called her back when I got in my car. "Yeah, Regina, what's up?" I asked her.

"You're never going to believe what just happened today." She proceeded to tell me about her visit to Harrison in prison. I got excited as she spoke, but not as excited as I should've been. My enthusiasm was muted by what I just did, and the fact that it was uncertain this entire plan would work anyway. I thought I had a fool-proof plan with my extortion idea. It boomeranged on me in the worst way.

I might never find out who killed Becky.

"Okay, listen, you keep me posted on the progress," I told her. "I want to know when the girls are safe to get out of that compound, and then I have to come up with a plan to get them out of there. We'll go from there. In the mean-time, I need you to do some research for me."

I told her about what Paul told me about Carl's airtight

alibi for Becky's murder. I needed her to verify that and she said she would.

———

I ARRIVED at my condo and was greeted by my two girls, Harlow and Lola, my beautiful boxer dogs. They were thrilled to see me, as usual, their tiny little docked tails wagging violently as they surrounded me. Harlow went and got her leash, which was hanging on the doorknob, brought it over to me and dropped it at my feet, and then went into a play bow, her butt up in the air, her front paws crouched down. Lola, for her part, dashed into the bedroom and brought out my tennis shoes in her mouth and dropped them at my feet.

In spite of myself, I had to smile and laugh at their antics. They were so smart. They knew the leash and tennis shoes meant they would go for a walk on the beach to see all their puppy friends.

"I see you girls are giving me some unsubtle hints about where you want to go." I went down the hall and knocked on Aidan's door. I knew he was home because the girls were home. My arrangement with him was to pick the dogs up at their doggie daycare when he was finished with his work for the day, if he finished before me. Since he usually got off right at 5 o'clock, and I usually worked later than that, he usually brought them home.

"Come in," he called when I knocked on his door.

I opened up the door and he was laying on his bed, a magazine in his hand. "Hey, what's up?" he asked me.

"Nothing. I just wanted you to know I'm home and I'm going to take the girls out for a walk."

"Cool. Hey, I saw on the Internet that that dude, that

Paul Sharpton dude, bought it. He jumped out the window."

I swallowed. "I know." I decided not to say anything else about it, because I was too raw, too numb. Aidan would find out in due time that I was present when Paul killed himself. But at that moment, I just couldn't talk about it.

"That's all you're going to say? You know? I mean, that guy ruined your life. I figured you'd be dancing a jig. Anyhow, if you'd like to smoke a bowl later on in celebration of that guy being wiped off the face of the earth, I'll be up for it."

I had to smile at that one. Aidan needed no excuse to smoke a bowl with me or anybody else.

"I just might take you up on it." And that was the truth. I didn't usually get into smoking marijuana. But, tonight, I would need something to take the edge off. There was just something about knowing you were responsible for a man's death that makes you really want to not look at yourself in the mirror ever again.

I got the leashes on the dogs and the three of us headed down to the beach. It was 7 o'clock, the end of a long day, and all I wanted to do was relax in front of the raging surf and try to forget what happened that day. It was strange, really. When I was laying in my prison bed, I dreamed about this guy's death. My fantasy was that he would die in a fire, or by drowning, or some other terrible way of going. I definitely didn't want him to have a painless death. I wanted it to be painful and protracted.

Yet now that his death was a reality, and I had to see it with my own eyes, and I knew I was the cause of it, it was different. My fantasies about getting back at him by making him die slowly were just that – fantasies.

I wondered if I could ever look at myself in the mirror again.

Chapter Eighteen

I MET with Regina the next evening. I would confess to her what I did. I had to tell somebody. Christian already knew, of course. After all, he was in on our entire scheme. He was my partner in crime, so to speak. He, like me, was stunned about what happened. About how it ended.

And, like me, he realized the implications of Paul taking the easy way out. That meant that there still was nobody to prosecute Carl's ring. It also meant the mystery as to who actually killed Becky would continue, because Regina looked into Carl's alibi for the time Becky was killed, and, just like Paul said, it was airtight. He was in Geneva, Switzerland, for an international conference. Regina did her due diligence, spoke with 10 people at that conference, and all of them confirmed Carl was there. She found, online, evidence that he had purchased a round-trip ticket, with the help of Christian's hacking. She found out the hotel he stayed at and he had signed in and out of that hotel.

So it seemed as if trying to convince somebody to prosecute Carl for Becky's murder wouldn't happen. But I still wasn't convinced his ring wasn't behind it. In fact, that was still my focus. I just knew Becky's death was somehow related to that ring.

The two of us met at Il Fornaio, an old-school Italian restaurant on the other side of the Hotel Del. It was an upscale place and Regina and I scored seat that looked out onto the ocean. Our seat was in an enclosed deck, with wicker chairs and white tablecloths on the table.

"What is it with you and fancy places?" Regina asked me when she walked into the restaurant.

"I don't know, I just like this place. My favorite thing is the Pollo Toscano." I was a purist, and the free range rosemary chicken combined with the potatoes and vegetables was something that was my idea of heaven.

Regina just shrugged. "Hey, there's pizza on the menu, so I'm all good." She scrunched up her nose as she looked at the menu. "But, even the pizzas are fancy here. White truffle oil on a pizza? Just throw some pepperoni on there and I'm good."

I pointed out the fradiovolo, a pizza with Italian sausage, mushrooms, bell peppers, red onions, and tomato sauce. She was right. The pizzas were fancy, but that particular one seemed the most traditional.

Regina nodded her head. "Yeah, that sounds good. Anyhow, you and I gotta talk about what our next move is." She then proceeded to tell me about her meeting with Harrison. "I want to see him tomorrow and see if he talked with his friend about getting Yuri out of that ring, and then I'm going to have to figure out if Yuri really is out. And if he is, we're golden. I'll admit, I was afraid that if I started rounding up the girls to get them out of there, Yuri would send his goons after me and them. I don't care if he sends his goons after me. But I didn't want to put their lives in danger. But take Yuri out of the formula and I think we can get them all out of there."

"Yes. And then it's just a matter of my filing a lawsuit against Carl. With the attendant publicity that such a case would garner, combined with the fact that his clients will be terrified they'll be exposed, I think that will be the nail in the coffin. Carl's going to have bottomless pockets to pay these girls, but that's really not the point. Sunlight is the point. That and the fact that the girls really need to be compensated. All of that's the point."

The waiter came around and took our order and I ordered a bottle of wine for the both of us. "Now on to our next problem. Carl obviously wasn't personally behind killing Becky. How can we figure out who was?"

Regina bit her bottom lip. "I don't know. I'll keep trying to turn over every rock in that place. Even if Carl himself wasn't behind it, I have a feeling somebody's gonna know what happened to her. I think that you and I agree that Carl might not have been directly behind it but his dirty paws were in there somewhere. We just have to figure out where."

"Okay. The first thing you need to do is to figure out if Yuri is out of Carl's orbit and if he is, you're going to have to figure out some way to talk to every one of those girls and make them feel comfortable with leaving. I know a lot of them probably are concerned about how they can live outside of that compound. I have to agree they are probably right to be worried about that. Some of the girls are runaways and might be returned to their parents. Others were on the street for other reasons. They'll have to go into the system. All of them are minors, and obviously the ones pressed into doing that by their parents will also have to go into the system. I know they're scared and won't want to do that but we have to convince them there really is not a choice."

"Well, hopefully, most of the girls will have some kind of a relative who might be able to take them in. I have to admit, I'm worried about every one of them," Regina said.

And then Regina told me Britney's story. It was probably one of the most heartbreaking stories I had ever heard in my life. "I feel badly for her as well. And I know that maybe for her, staying at that Carl compound would be the lesser of two evils. But we're going to have to figure it out. Anyhow, I think we have to come up with a plan to make this entire thing foolproof. In other words, we have to make it to where the business collapses on itself. And then Carl will ask all the girls to leave."

As Regina and I enjoyed our delicious Italian food by the sea, we hashed out a plan I thought was a good one. If everything worked out, getting the girls out of there would be a cinch. What happened next, of course, with the girls' situation, was anybody's guess. But it had to be better than what they were doing now.

Chapter Nineteen

THE NEXT WEEK, I found out from Regina that Yuri had, in fact, dropped Carl as a client. "We better strike while the iron's hot or at least while Carl does not have an enforcer behind him. It's only a matter of time before he finds somebody else to take over the job that Yuri was doing and our window will shut on our fingers."

So I found myself scheduled to go to Carl's mansion. I made an appointment with him, telling him that I was being sent to try to clean up the situation. At that point, Carl apparently was running around like a chicken with its head cut off, trying desperately to find somebody else who would run interference for him in the outside world. I had the unenviable task of telling Carl the jig was up, there was nowhere to turn and it was time to pack it in.

But the day before I was scheduled to go to Carl's place, I got a phone call from Regina. "Listen, I need you to come over here. I got this guy over here at my house. I need you to check him out. If you can check him out, it might help matters."

"What guy is that?"

"His name is Ari Romo. Listen, it's a long story, but I've been seeing a guy at Carl's place. He told me his name was something else, but his name is actually Ari Romo. He's been telling me who he really is, and frankly, I'm not sure if I believe him. But, like I say, if we can get this guy on our side, if he's legit, then it's really going to help."

"And he's at your condo right now?"

"Yeah. Listen, I don't know how he did it, but he got my phone number. We talked a lot on the phone last night and I invited him over. And now I want you to meet him."

"Okay. I'll be right over."

———

SO I HEADED down to Regina's Imperial Beach condo. Her condo was situated right on the beach as well, just like mine. I thought her place was cute and funky, just like her. It had hardwood floors, modern art on all the walls, a dining room with a distressed wood table and leather chairs, and a fireplace with a big-screen television above the mantel. She also had a balcony that faced the surf below. Her condo was smaller than mine, but that was because she was only one person living there and I had my brother living with me.

At any rate, her place was definitely her.

When I got there, there was a guy sitting out on the balcony with her. He had sandy blonde hair and dark eyes with long eyelashes. He was a handsome guy, long and lean and dressed in a very fashionable manner. Blue jeans, leather shoes, a light tweed jacket even though it was currently 80°, and a light purple button down. He was sitting very casually out on the balcony, his right foot over his left knee. When he saw me come in, he stood up and smiled and gave me his hand.

"Avery? Name's Ari Romo. Regina was just telling me that you were coming over and she was telling me she wants me to meet you. I'm a reporter with the New York *Times*."

I looked over at Regina and she just shrugged. "Hey, I've been seeing this dude at these parties at least once a week, sitting around and not doing much. He paid his dues just like everybody else and I'm guessing that there's not much vetting going on of the people who come in that place. I mean, as long as you got the $50,000 to plunk down, they're going to let you in the door. And, well, the paper apparently gave him that money. He's been working on this story for months. And I found out that the last time I was at the prison, talking to Harrison Baker, the guy who was involved in the Aslanian clan, this guy found out why I was there. He was also there, just by coincidence, talking to one of his confidential informants in another case. He found out who I was talking to and went to talk to him as well and he found out what was going on. He was on top of the story like white on rice because he sees an opening for himself as well."

He smiled when she said that. "Yeah. I've been working on that story for all this time, but I admit, I was afraid I would get killed because of Yuri being involved with Carl. My editor apparently got a message from Yuri last month about me. He figured out who I was and he was making threats to the newspaper about what would happen if I went ahead with the story. And it wouldn't be pretty. Not that that scares the paper. The paper obviously publishes stories all the time where there's threats being made against them, but they go ahead with the story anyway. But the editor was afraid for my life so she was sitting on it for now. But Regina managed to get Yuri out of the picture, so it's now time for me to strike as well. And I can be extremely valuable to you if you allow me to go with you to talk to Carl. I already have my story written up and I know exactly who has been in that place over the last six months. And the best part? I have a client list. Don't ask me how I got it, but I have it."

"So you already have what you need to file the story?"

"The story's already been written. So if you take me with you, I can be very persuasive in convincing him that he needs to hang it up. The only problem is that he might flee the scene. But then again, that wouldn't be tragic, because nobody has been able to prosecute him yet. And trust me, in my story I'm going to expose everybody who has been in this guy's pocket, which is just about every judge, prosecutor, and cop you can imagine. In other words, nobody's going to charge him with a crime here. So if he decides to flee to someplace else, I guess he's going to be their problem. Not that that makes me feel good. I would obviously prefer that this guy can't hurt other girls anywhere in the world, but once this story comes out in the newspaper, the entire world will be on notice as to exactly what kind of person he is. Something tells me that even if he decides to flee the scene and go to a different country, he won't be able to do what he's doing anymore with impunity."

I suddenly started to get excited as I talked to this guy. Everything was coming together. I knew there was a good chance that by the end of this week, Carl would be a hunted man. Everybody in his pocket would look like the chicken shits they were and Carl would be exposed. Best of all, it meant Carl would shut down his operation and all those girls would be asked to leave. Regina had become close with every girl who had lived there and she had even become close with the day players, which meant I hopefully could sign all of them up for a lawsuit against Carl. That would be the final nail in the coffin and those girls could finally get a bit of justice for the childhood taken from them.

"Okay. You come with me when I talk to Carl tomorrow. I'm supposed to see him at two. He thinks I'm going to help him with the task of finding somebody else to be his enforcer. At least that's the story I gave him."

———

SO, the next day, Ari and I ended up driving up to Del Mar to Carl's mansion. Just like Regina had said, the place was gorgeous. It was a modernist home, all glass and steel and cubes and looked like the home of a Hollywood star. There wasn't anybody at the gate, no guy with a gun like when Regina first went there. I simply spoke into the intercom, explained who I was, and they buzzed me on through.

I drove up the long drive to the front door and Ari and I got out of the car and went up to the enormous wooden door and rang the bell. A guy answered the door.

"Hello, my name is Jurgen. I'm Carl's son. You must be Avery." He looked over at Ari. "You can't be here. I know who you are and what you're doing and you can't be here."

We were prepared for this. "On the contrary, I am going to be here," Ari said. "And who's gonna stop me? I happen to know Carl does not have a goon who will stop me from being in here and we need to talk to your dad today. We need to tell him what's going to happen. We need to talk to him about what his next step will be. Now you need to let us in the door, because we both need to talk to him."

Jurgen looked at me and shook his head. "You lied to me over the phone. I should've known. But come on back, I have a feeling that there is not a whole lot we can do to avoid the coming storm. My father couldn't find backup enforcement, so I'll be honest, he's screwed. I didn't know he was screwed until just now, but I have a feeling I know the reason you guys are here."

I could see in the guy's eyes that he wished he could kill both of us right there. But he also knew that would be pointless. He had to have known that Ari's story would run and if Ari turned up dead, the first person that anybody would be looking at would be Carl himself.

He led us down the hall, out onto an enormous deck facing a cliff. I could see distant ships on the water. Sitting in a chair, in front of a long glass table, was a man of about 55. He was in decent shape, extremely handsome, with dimples and blue eyes. However, even though he smiled at me when I walked out to meet him, I could tell in those blue eyes that he was very troubled. He took one look at Ari next to me and his face fell.

"You!" He said, pointing right at Ari. "I trusted you. I let you in here, I let you have free rein of anything you wanted. You drank my alcohol, you ate my food, you had fun at all my parties. I never thought one of my clients would stab me in the back the way you apparently have."

Ari just smiled. "I might've been at all your parties, but I never once touched any of the girls there. I'm sorry that didn't ring alarm bells in your head, but, frankly, I'm surprised it didn't. I'm sorry you trusted me but you're responsible for my being in here in the first place. If you would've done some proper vetting, instead of just letting anybody in the door who had the exorbitant sum you charged for the vile things you were doing, I would've never gotten in the front door."

Then he looked at me. He figured out I wasn't who I was and he looked like he wanted to kill me on the spot. "You're here with him, so obviously you're not who you said you were either. So, out with it. Who are you and what do you really want?"

"Okay. I'm here to warn you about what's about to happen," I said. "As you probably have figured out, Ari here has written a story about your operation. It's going to be filed in the New York *Times* any day. And there's no way you can kill the story because you don't have the manpower to do so anymore. After Yuri left you, you were left without the means to make people do what you want. Oh, I know you have everybody in town in your pocket. I know you have every judge and prosecutor and cop in your pocket, and you have information on all of them to blackmail them if you can't bribe them. I understand that. But you got nothing on me and got nothing on Ari. And I'm here to tell you that time's up."

"Time is up," I repeated. "You don't scare me. You can't do anything to me. I've been to prison and there's not much that can scare me anymore. So listen up, because here's what's gonna happen. Ari will file his story and he has your client list. He's going to publish it in the newspaper. It's gonna be a scandalous story to end all scandalous stories. Everybody who's been participating in these sick acts will be exposed for the sickos they are. The game is over. Now I want you to explain to all the girls in this house that you are letting all of them go. You really have no choice in the matter. The story comes out, you're going to be a hunted man, and so will all the people who have visited this place."

I watched his face and could see he knew he was defeated. He had no goons to back him up. He had nothing on me he could blackmail me with. He could get nothing on me to blackmail me with, either. His dirty deeds would be broadcast to the entire world.

There wasn't a thing he could do. He was finally going to be brought to justice. Not in the legal sense, because he probably still wouldn't end up in prison due to his "connections." But in the real sense that everybody would know about him, he would be hated around the world, and Netflix specials were no doubt going to be aired about him - he was done. Finished. Cooked.

He narrowed his eyes. "Do what you will. I'll never stand trial for this. Understand that now. And, just so you know, I might be unprotected at this time, but there are plenty of families who would be willing to work with me. Plenty of them. I just haven't found time to recruit one because Yuri left me in the lurch. But when I do find one, you better watch your back. I have ways of making people dance to my tune and I'll stop at nothing to destroy you if you destroy me. You got that? I will bury you."

"Huh," I said. "Where have I heard that before? Sorry, not scared. I'm long past being afraid of small men like you. Now, you *are* going to have a talk with all of your girls and you're going to tell each one that their services are no longer necessary. I'm afraid you don't have a choice in that matter."

Carl refused to meet my eyes. "The girls will be released from my service by the end of the day."

"I thought so."

_____

BY THE END of the day, each girl was given their walking papers. Regina was there to protect them. Britney was the girl who called her first, and she told her that all the other girls would soon be doing the same. They all were scared. They had the rug pulled out from under them. They hated what they did for Carl, absolutely despised it, but they had become a family to one another during their months of captivity. They had to rely on one another for all that time and they would all be scattered to the wind.

Regina invited Britney to her home and asked her to bring the others as well. She and I came up with the idea of renting out a large home in the North Park area of town. The rent was $10,000 a month, but the place was enormous - six bedrooms, four bathrooms, a living room, den, dining room and enormous sun room. Regina's place was obviously too small for the girls to live in and so was my place. Regina knew that none of the girls had a place to go. Either they were runaways because their home life was intolerable, filled with abuse, both sexual and physical, or they were pressed into service by their mother or father. None of the girls were kidnapped from a good home. They all had horrors to relate.

I was faced with a dilemma with all of them. If I alerted the authorities to their presence, they would be taken into the system. Some of them would be returned to parents who beat them, starved them, raped them. The rest would become foster kids or put into a group home. I didn't want that for any of them. I wanted to keep them together. They had become each other's support system and I didn't want to break that up.

I would be doing something illegal if I just kept them in that large home, with Regina and I taking turns staying there with them. But that was what I was tempted to do. At the same time, I knew they all needed to re-enroll in school and try to get their lives back on track. If they did that, if they re-enrolled in school, the jig would be up.

So, I arranged a meeting with a social worker who might be able to help me find a way around this particular situation. But, for now, the girls were safe in this large home. There were 20 of them, all survivors of a particularly heinous war.

———

THE NEXT EVENING, after the girls got settled into the house, I called a meeting with them. I would have to tell them about the lawsuit I planned to file on their behalf, and explain to them what I was going to have to do, as far as calling the social worker. When I talked about that, I saw fear in all of their eyes.

"I don't want to leave this place," Naomi, a gorgeous cafe *au lait* Jamaican girl cried, her enormous brown eyes filled with tears. "These other girls, they're my sisters now. If you call the social worker, I'm going to be placed with an abusive family like my last foster family was. They locked me in a closet while they went out with their friends. They had other kids in that house and they were all locked in a closet, too. They didn't want to find a sitter for us, even a respite sitter, and they didn't always have food in the house, either."

I heard story after story like that.

"I'm sorry, girls, I really am, but all of you have to get back into school. You all have to get your diploma if you ever hope to become something in this world. And you can't get back into school unless the system is notified about your situation. I'm really sorry. I would do anything if I could find a way that all of you could stay together and still go to school, but I just don't see any way for that to happen."

After I spoke with all of them, however, I knew that I was going to have to make it happen.

No matter what, I would make it happen.

Chapter Twenty

WHEN I MET with a social worker about the girls, she gave me an idea. Her name was Elaine Suffolk and she was a heavy-set woman with a tight perm and a ready smile. "I'll put you in touch with individuals licensed to run a group home," she said. "If you can hire somebody to run it for you, and staff it with the professionals necessary for the girls, you might be able to keep them together. I'll have to meet with all the girls and make sure they're eligible for this situation. I'm sorry, but we're probably going to have to contact their parents, but for the girls who were already in the system before they were brought to that home in Del Mar, it will be easy to get them placed in this home. I'll have to do an investigation of all of their situations and make a recommendation to the court. I'll get it expedited, because this is an urgent situation, and hopefully we can keep all these girls together in that home."

That was encouraging to me. Most of the girls were in the system already, having been taken away from their birth parents long ago. The one girl I was concerned about was

Britney, however. Her parents were in New York and her father was a respected judge. She ran away from home because nobody would believe her claims of abuse at the hands of her father. She would probably have to go home and I was afraid for her.

I put the fate of the girls in the hands of the social worker, however. She would take the necessary steps to make sure each of the girls were eligible to stay in the home I rented out. She gave me some referrals for people licensed to run group homes and I immediately got to work interviewing them.

By the end of two weeks, all of the girls were formally placed in the home together, even Britney. I found an excellent person to run and staff the home. Her name was Stella Gerwig and she had years of experience. Within another few weeks, everything was running smoothly and all the girls were back in school. They were all working with therapists who were helping them with their traumas, both before and after they started working in Carl's house of horrors.

The way Britney was able to live with the others was that Elaine got in touch with social workers in New York. Apparently, after Britney ran away from home, her father, the "respected" federal judge, ended up in a federal prison after he was caught taking bribes from local politicians. Her mother was then committed to a mental institution, where she remained. It was determined that Britney didn't have any relatives willing to take her in so Elaine got her placed in the home as well.

IN THE MEANTIME, Carl absconded to his home in Sweden to get away from the absolute storm of publicity that happened after Ari filed his story in the New York *Times*. It was the top story for weeks on end. Every tabloid, social media feed and 24-hour news channel was filled with story after story about what the girls went through in that home. Nobody could believe that something like that could happen in America - and the *Times* boldly published his client list. Everybody on the list threatened lawsuits but these threats were empty. These men knew what they did. They were shunned by society from that point on. Many jurisdictions were filing criminal charges against them. They were all ruined.

I wasn't satisfied with any of it. I still didn't know who killed Becky, for one thing. For another, it didn't seem fair that Carl could get away on his private jet and live someplace else because everybody in America absolutely despised him. The judges, cops and prosecutors all had to answer for why they didn't prosecute him, even though all of this was happening under their noses. All the men who were Carl's clients were suffering.

Why shouldn't Carl also feel pain?

I had to get a lawsuit going against him. I would win in court if he decided to fight me, which he probably would. I didn't want to settle the case, either. I wanted him subpoenaed and wanted him to tell the world about what he did. I wanted him to squirm on the witness stand. Bringing him back to answer for this lawsuit wouldn't be easy but I would do it.

The girls needed that closure. They also could use the money that would come from this suit. I also wanted justice.

Justice for the girls.

And justice for Becky.

Chapter Twenty-One

I WAS OVERWHELMED with everything that I would have to do to get this lawsuit off the ground. There were witnesses to contact, mainly people who worked for Carl - the staff, the cooks, and Jacqueline Price, the house mother. I would get all of them in for depositions, but first I needed to talk to the prosecutor's office about whether these people would be charged with anything. I thought it would be appropriate if they would be charged - they let it all happen, after all - but, at the same time, I thought that it would be an abomination that they would go to prison and Carl the snake would not.

However, I contacted the prosecutor and they said they had no plans on filing charges against anybody working for Carl in an adjunct way. The prosecutor told me they could consider filing charges regarding aiding and abetting, but that was a long shot, so they would just leave it alone.

I knew Carl would hire a hardball attorney, and, when I filed the case, I knew that I was right when I got a phone call from one Jonathan Augusto.

Jonathan was known not just as an attorney but also as a fixer. He was the guy you called when you needed somebody shady and unethical to defend you in a lawsuit. When you needed people threatened. I knew him as the fixer to the stars - his practice was based in Los Angeles - and he was known as the guy who covered up many Hollywood stars' various misdeeds. It was rumored that one particular A-Lister accidentally hit and killed a young boy while this A-Lister was three sheets to the wind. Jonathan quietly paid the family of the boy millions of dollars of hush money. Another movie producer was well-known around town to like young boys. Once a tabloid reporter followed this guy and threatened to file a story about it, Jonathan knocked the tabloid reporter in the head and threw a dead prostitute in his bed with him and took pictures. The prostitute wasn't actually murdered by Jonathan, at least not that I knew of. She was found in the dumpster, just another statistic, and Jonathan was "lucky" enough to have found her in time to place that dead prostitute in the reporter's bed and threaten him with going to the police about it if the reporter didn't kill the story.

The reporter killed the story.

That was the kind of attorney he was. He would do everything underhanded possible to make sure his client didn't have to answer for his crimes. I knew that going in and was prepared for it.

"Ms. Collins," he said when he called me. "I've entered my appearance on behalf of Carl Williams. You will regret the day you decided to file a case against him. That much I know. I don't think you know who you're dealing with here. I really don't. But you're about to find out. Fuck around and find out. That's all I can say to you."

"You don't scare me. Here's what I say to you. Carl

might have escaped prosecution because he threatened to break more than a few kneecaps around town, metaphorically speaking, but he won't escape being brought to justice in a court of law. Not if I can help it."

"It's your funeral. You have a nice life and I'll see you in court."

I nodded. "Since we've established that I won't back down from this, what you and I need to talk about is exchanging discovery. I already have his client list. I know exactly who was going in and out of that place. I'll be sending you some interrogatories and request for production of documents, so be looking out for them. And just like you said that I should have a nice life, I think you should also have a nice life. I refuse to be intimidated by you or anybody else."

"Okay. I gave you fair warning. Expect my opening shot sometime this week. I won't just tell you to expect it soon because I want to give you a time frame. My exact time frame is, oh, say, tomorrow by noon. You'll soon find out what I mean."

I hung up the phone without even saying goodbye. And then I got to work on my document and interrogatory requests and also got to work with preparing some subpoenas for depositions. One of the people I wanted to depose, of course, was Ari himself. He was invaluable to me. Like Regina, he had been to party after party and he understood what was going on. The girls would be my best witnesses, of course. While Ari could testify about what happened outside the bedroom, the girls could testify about what happened inside it. I had already talked to them and it wasn't pretty.

A part of me didn't want to put them through it. I knew

the media glare would be intense on this case, to say the very least. While they were minors, therefore the media wasn't allowed to disclose any information about them to the public, and there would be no way the judge would consent to having cameras in the courtroom, I knew the names of the girls were out there in the media. Their names were on X, Meta, Instagram, Tik Tok, every manner of social media there was. A part of me felt absolutely sick the girls would be put through a court case. They were all on board for it, of course. They were learning from their therapist exactly how exploited they were and were eager to bring Carl to justice, just as I was.

But I still had a nagging feeling that everything would go completely wrong.

───────

THE NEXT DAY, just before noon, I found out exactly what the pig-of-a-man Jonathan Augusto was talking about. I was in my law office, minding my own business, when the cops showed up at my door.

"Is your name Avery Collins?" one of the cops asked me. His badge indicated his name was Officer Silva, and the other officer's name was McDonald.

"Yes. That's my name. What's this about?"

"Ma'am, you have to come with me. We got an anonymous tip from an established and well-regarded informant that you are in possession of cocaine. We got a warrant to search your vehicle in the covered parking of this building and found this." At that, Officer Silva produced a large bag of cocaine. "I'm afraid you're going to have to come with us."

I looked at the bag of cocaine in the guy's hand and just shook my head. Jonathan was up to his dirty tricks. However, he didn't know who he was messing with.

He didn't know at all.

Chapter Twenty-Two

ANONYMOUS MAN

Fall of 1998

THE MAN KNEW that he had his pick of young girls. Every night he was able to see a veritable smorgasbord of young nubile women. Not that they were interested in him. He knew they weren't. After all, in their eyes, he was nobody. Nobody at all.

Yet he knew in his mind that he was somebody. He was somebody very important and they just didn't realize it. But he knew there would come a time when they would realize it.

In the meantime, he knew there was a way he could have all of them. But he really didn't want all of them. He only wanted the one.

Becky Whitfield.

He'd seen her laying around the pool at a party one night. She wasn't necessarily the most beautiful woman in the place. Or even the most beautiful girl in the place.

Because, after all, at her age, she was considered to be a girl, not a woman. He always had to remind himself of that.

A girl, not a woman.

Yet there was something about her that drew him right into her orbit. He wasn't even sure what it was. Maybe it was the way she smiled at him. When she looked at him, it really seemed she was smiling genuinely. Not because she wanted something from him but because she wanted to be friendly.

He was always concerned the girls were wanting to get to know him because they were trying to get at somebody else. They all wanted something from him, something he wasn't willing to give them. But not Becky. She was genuinely friendly with him and showed an interest.

Because she was so nice, he decided that, one night, when she was over at his house, he would share something with her. He had a stash of cocaine in his bedroom. She was shy at first, telling him she had never seen a drug like that.

"I smoke pot all the time," Becky said. "With my friends. I mean, they all do it. But I don't really want to do another drug. Not something serious, not something like cocaine."

He wasn't listening to her. He knew that when she got going with it, she would be like all the others. He heard the protestations of other girls in her same situation. Girls he had asked to do some lines with him. Half of the girls were eager to try it but the other half were very reluctant. They heard all about how their brain would be on drugs, and all about how addiction is, and some of them had even seen their parents get addicted. But, to a girl, he was able to talk all of them into doing coke with him. And they all really started to like it. And once they started to like it, and they knew he could give it to them, he was able to get other favors from them. Especially the ones who became addicted after one snort. Those were the girls he liked the best. He could get them to do anything for him. He only had to give them the drug.

That was how he managed to get along, sexually, in the world. He had something to provide. Something people really wanted. And he knew that all that he needed to do with Becky was show her the way.

So instead of listening to what she had to say, he simply snorted a line right in front of her. And then he gave the mirror, with the four lines of coke on it, to her. "Trust me on this. Once you snort that, you'll feel like superwoman. It's a high like you have never experienced. I'm telling you, man, if you don't do this with me, you're missing out."

He saw her resolve crumble right before his very eyes. "Okay. I'm curious about it. I suppose it wouldn't hurt, just to do it this just this once."

There you go. I knew you would come around.

She leaned down with the straw in her nose and snorted one line. And then, for good measure, she snorted another. Then she sat back on the couch and shook her head.

Her eyes got very wide. "Whoa. Whoa whoa whoa whoa whoa."

The other thing he liked about the girls getting high with him was that they were much more willing to give him what he wanted while in the euphoric state. It was time to make his move.

However, Becky wasn't up for it. "What are you doing?" she asked when he immediately tried to feel up her breast. He then tried to unbuckle her pants, clumsily putting one hand on the buckle and one hand down her pants.

She shook her head and kicked him in his stomach. "Stop that. I'm serious. Stop it."

He had had several lines before she ever got into the room and when she told him to stop, and then kicked him, it enraged him beyond measure. He slapped her, which only made her kick him again.

"Listen, you bitch," he said to her. "You can only get this stuff from me. I got the good stuff. You try to get that shit off the street, they'll be cutting it with rat poison. That won't just make your nose bleed, it'll make your intestines bleed. You'll be shitting out blood for a week. So you'll be back. I know you'll be back, and sooner or later, you're going to give me what I want from you. I can guarantee that."

She just shook her head and walked out the door, slamming it in his face.

But he knew she would be back. She would always come back, anyhow, of that he knew. But he also knew for sure that she would come back to his bedroom. She would understand that the drugs he was supplying her were top-of-the-line, better than anything she could get anyplace else. And she would come back begging him.

It was just a matter of time.

———

AND SHE DID COME BACK a few months later.

He once again tried to force himself on her. But she wasn't there for the drugs. She was there to tell him to leave her the hell alone. She had already told him that over the phone and now she had to tell him in person.

He couldn't stand to hear those words from her. He was high on coke and agitated as it was. She was the girl of his fantasies, and here she was, telling him she didn't want to see him anymore.

Before he knew it, he was on top of her, stripping her jeans off and forcing himself inside of her. When she screamed, he wanted her to stop, so he he punched her in the face and kicked her in the stomach. She still wouldn't be quiet, so he put his hands around her neck and squeezed hard. He was confused. He thought his hands were on her mouth. He only wanted her to be quiet.

He only wanted her to be quiet.

And she was. He ejaculated inside of her and then he noticed she wasn't moving. Or breathing.

She was dead.

He didn't know how she died. He didn't do that, did he? But he knew he did.

Just then, somebody came into his apartment.

He went out onto the balcony and started down the fire escape, but not before he saw who was in his place.

It was her friend. That Avery Collins. She must have been waiting for her outside in her car.

She saw what happened and screamed.

And that's all he knew. Before he knew it, he was down the fire escape and calling his dad. His dad could fix it. He fixed everything.

He hoped.

Chapter Twenty-Three

AVERY

IN THE BACK of the squad car, I was seething inside. What was it about me that made people want to frame me for shit I didn't do? Here I was, apparently the victim of Jonathan planting drugs in my car, and he probably got some kind of source who the police knew well to call in a tip about it. I knew something about anonymous tips and I knew cops don't usually use them as a basis for a search warrant unless the tipster is someone they knew. They would try to get corroborating evidence if it was somebody they didn't know.

Jonathan warned me. He warned me to be looking out for an opening salvo, and sure enough, just like he said, it came. It came in the form of my going to the station to answer some questions about some cocaine I knew nothing about. It was so ironic, once I thought about it. I had been anti-drug my entire life. I only partook in marijuana once in awhile and that was only because it was legal. I never tried anything other than marijuana in my entire life. I had always been a straight arrow, even in prison, where drugs were abundant. And yet, here I was, going downtown in the back of a cop car, because of what?

Possession of cocaine.

I was taken down to the jail and processed in, all the while thinking it was home sweet home. I had gone through all of this rigmarole before. I knew the ropes. They would fingerprint me, take my mug shot, swab my mouth for DNA, take my information, and throw me into a freezing cell. I would be in that cell for hours before being allowed to call my attorney. In this case, I knew my attorney would be Christian. I would've called my brother, Aidan, but I knew that he would just laugh his ass off about my being in this predicament. Because that was the kind of person he was. He would find this incredibly funny.

ABOUT AN HOUR after I arrived there, after I was put through all manner of indignity, I was thrown into a cold cell. I was there with five other women. Most of them looked like they really were in there for drug possession, but a couple of them looked like they were in there for prostitution. Most of them looked at me with wary eyes, but one girl came up to me and was very friendly.

"You don't look like you should be in here," she said. She was dressed in a tight dress, low-cut on top, high cut on the bottom. She had reddish blonde hair, straight with a streak of blue running towards the middle of it. She had bare feet, but I could see in the corner of the cell a pair of high heels thrown on the floor.

I sighed. I really wasn't in the mood to talk to anybody.

"I don't belong here. I really don't. I got on the wrong side of somebody ruthless. I'm an attorney."

She smiled and nodded. "I thought I recognized you. You were on TV. You're the girl defending that poor Hispanic maid who was framed for killing that rich girl. All my friends were telling me they thought she did it. But I knew she didn't. Turned out it was that rich bastard, wasn't it?"

"Yep. It certainly was." I wasn't sure how I felt about being recognized in the jail. It was embarrassing, in a way. It was humiliating to be an attorney in the clink. These other the ladies in jail probably didn't care what I was. To say the least. Yet I was still embarrassed.

"Yeah. And I guess you're also the one put in prison all those years ago for something you didn't do. I remember. I read all about that online. Weren't they even going to make a Netflix special about you or something? I think I remember reading about that."

"Well it was going to be for Court TV. And, yes, after the Esme Gutierrez case, I was approached with offers to make my story into a Netflix special. But I didn't want that to happen. I wanted to shut the door on all that."

Her eyes got wide when I said that. "Close the door on being famous? Oh my God, I would love to be famous. For any reason. I would love to be rich, too. I bet you're rich, aren't you?"

I took a deep breath. It was clear this girl wouldn't leave me alone, no matter how many nonverbal cues I was giving her that I wanted just that. "Yes, I am rich. However I'm only rich because I was thrown in prison for seven years and I sued the state of Missouri, or should I say Misery, for doing that to me. I sued and won a boatload of money. I was able to show corruption with the prosecutor all day long."

"I know what you mean. I'm being falsely persecuted all the time. Listen, I'm a hairdresser. I don't know why I'm always being picked up for being a working girl. I think maybe I got on the wrong side of somebody, too. Maybe you and me, we got stuff in common, huh?"

"Maybe."

"So who was behind murdering your friend, all those years ago? Did you ever figure that out?"

"No. I mean, I thought I was on the right track, but it turned out I wasn't."

"Who did you think did it?" she asked.

"A guy by the name of Carl Williams. I'm sure you read about him in the paper." This girl seem to be pretty up on all the latest scandalous gossip.

The girl shook her head. "Oh my God, what was that all about? I mean, come on, what a sicko. I dated his son for a little while and let's just say the apple don't fall too far from the tree with that family. I mean, Jurgen, he's a bit of a psycho himself. I had to get a restraining order against him because he was stalking me. Turned out he stalks just about every girl he dates. Can't take no for an answer. But, oh my God, what his dad was doing, that's just wrong."

My ears perked up when she was talking about Carl's son. "Jurgen? What do you know about Jurgen?" Regina had mentioned Jurgen from time to time. She said that he was Carl's son and apparently he was a wealthy man in his own right. He didn't hang out around the house all that often, just once or twice, and Regina never saw him actually participate in any of the parties. Regina had no reason to suspect that Jurgen was anybody she should be looking into, but maybe, after talking to this girl, she should be.

The girl just shrugged. "By the way, my name is Naomi. And I know you're Avery Collins. You're like a total rock star, just so you know."

I felt flattered, but I was mainly just very intensely curious about what she could tell me about this Jurgen person. "Tell me more about his son."

"What is there to tell? We went out a couple of times and I decided I didn't like him. I mean, he's a good looking guy, he's loaded, but there's just something very off about him. Besides, my boyfriend Vinnie, he came back in the picture. He ain't in the picture no more, but that's besides the point. He came back in the picture back then, and Jurgen, he just didn't like me telling him we couldn't see each other no more. So, you know, he came around the house all the time. He'd wait until he saw Vinnie's car outside my apartment – I live in Ocean Beach in an apartment – and he'd come up to the door and start screaming at me. And one time, he had sex with me, even though I told him I wasn't wanting to see him anymore. He like came into my apartment and just kinda just ripped off my clothes, threw me on the bed and did it to me. After that, I got a restraining order. I guess he moved on, because I ain't heard from him since."

"Did he ever threaten you? Did he ever make you think he was going to kill you?"

Naomi looked into the distance as she was trying to think about my question. Her eyes were scrunched up, her posture was slumped, and she was focusing on a tiny crack in the cement wall. "Yeah. He did. He put his hands around my neck that last time, when he –"

"When he raped you, right?"

"Yeah. I guess so. I mean, he told me he couldn't rape me because we were dating at one time. I was pretty sure that wasn't how it worked, but he told me that once I agreed to have sex with him one time, that meant he could have sex with me anytime he wanted to. A lot of people think you can't rape someone you're dating or married to. Did you know that?"

"I'm very familiar with that idea, unfortunately. But, as you probably know, that's not true. A husband can rape a wife and a boyfriend can rape a girlfriend. In your case, he wasn't even your boyfriend at the time, so that really was a case of rape. But I'm sorry I interrupted you. What were you saying earlier?"

"What was the question again?" she asked.

"You were saying something about Jurgen putting his hands around your throat when he raped you."

"Oh, yeah. Right. He raped me and he put his hands around my throat. And I thought he was going to kill me. I really did. I even blacked out. Everything was blackness and I was scared to death. But something must've happened because I'm still alive. Still alive, and still getting brought in for things I don't do."

I suddenly realized that I had to get out of that cell. I realistically knew that I couldn't call Christian for hours after being put in the cell, and that it probably would be hours after that before I could bond out. It was currently 2 o'clock in the afternoon and I knew it would be at least midnight before I was out of there. But I was anxious to get going on this case. I couldn't believe I actually overlooked this Jurgen person. And that Regina did as well. This guy must not have been giving off too much of an evil vibe, otherwise Regina would've been on him like white on rice.

FOUR HOURS LATER, I was finally able to call Christian. "Christian, I'm in jail. That rat bastard Jonathan Augusto was as good as his word. He apparently planted some cocaine in my car and then got an informant to call the cops to search my car and the cops found a large bag of coke. I need for you to bond me out but I probably won't be out of here before midnight. I need for you to call Regina and ask her to do some research on Jurgen Williams. He's Carl son. I need to know if he was ever arrested, and if he was, if his DNA was given to the cops. And then I'm going to have to have his DNA compared to the DNA found inside of Becky when she died. I just have a feeling Carl was behind the prosecutor railroading me. Carl obviously didn't do it, but he was covering for somebody who did."

"On it. Listen, I'll bond you out. Hopefully you'll be out of there soon."

"Yeah. Hopefully soon. Just make sure Regina gets on this. It's very important."

I took a deep breath after I called Christian. I just had this hunch that Jurgen was behind killing Becky all those years ago. Carl would have covered for him. Wouldn't he have?

The only thing was, how could I get anybody to prosecute him for it? The murder was so long ago. Carl must've really leaned hard onto the prosecutor to make sure he didn't finger his son for anything. Paul, all those years ago, was prosecuting small time cases in Kansas City, Missouri. He was lured to San Diego by Carl himself and Carl's promise of endless young women for him to enjoy. Of course, it had to have been even more sinister than that. Carl knew how to push Paul's buttons all those years ago.

But Paul wasn't the prosecutor in Kansas City, Missouri, any more. Somebody else was. Maybe somebody who wasn't as compromised as Paul was. At any rate, Carl didn't have the same kind of power he did back then. I knew that if I got some pretty good evidence that this Jurgen person raped Becky, I might be able to convince them to reopen the case and nail him to the wall.

Chapter Twenty-Four

REGINA

REGINA GOT the call from Christian about Jurgen. She immediately kicked herself because she should've known there was something wrong with that guy. Her first instinct was that something was a bit off about him, but she only saw him a few times and didn't really think much about him. But she should have. If she would have, she would've been on him like white on rice.

The first thing she did was go through arrest records and found out that he was arrested. Surprisingly enough, considering who his father was. It was probably one of those things where the dad let him get arrested because he wanted to teach him a lesson. She found out that during Jurgen's arrest, which was for a DWI in San Diego, he gave DNA. This arrest happened two years ago which explained why there was no DNA on file that matched the DNA found inside of Becky at the time of Avery's trial and her retrial.

Other than that arrest, Regina didn't see that he had been arrested for anything else. Surprisingly enough. Considering the fact that he apparently was a violent person, she figured there might be other arrests lurking about. That made her more convinced than ever that the one arrest he did have for the DWI was just to teach him a lesson. There was just no way a stalky kind of person who goes around raping and strangling women would go his entire life with only one relatively minor infraction.

Then it was just a matter of matching up the guy's DNA with the DNA found inside of Becky, and she figured that maybe that would be enough evidence to get the case reopened. At the very least. She personally thought it was an open and shut case. It wouldn't be difficult for a prosecutor worth his or her salt to show that Paul was evidently compromised by Carl. After all, his name was on the client list that had been circulating around the Internet. It would be pretty simple to show that A led to B. Paul was a pedophile dying to get his kicks with real girls and Carl offered him a veritable smorgasbord of what he was craving, in exchange for Paul nailing somebody else for Becky's murder. It was just too neat of a scenario. It would fit beautifully into a very neat box.

Regina figured Avery was wrong about Paul. Avery had assumed that there wasn't necessarily a *quid pro quo* between the two of them, Carl and Paul. When she found out that Paul had his own money to pay for the admission into Carl's sick world, and she found out that Carl had an airtight alibi for the murder, she figured there wasn't a tit for tat involved in the situation. Granted, she knew, as did Regina, that Carl must've put a bug in Paul's ear about his little sick ranch in Del Mar, which was why Paul came out to San Diego in the first place. But the inherent *quid pro quo* was dismissed by Avery when it was discovered about Carl's alibi.

Now it was time for Regina to connect the dots again.

The dots that were not connected earlier when it was assumed that Carl had nothing to do with Becky's murder.

So the first thing she did was contact the Medical Examiner's Office in Kansas City, Missouri. She made an appointment with the medical examiner there, explaining what she needed. She knew the medical examiner was clean in this case and not involved in the cover-up. There was a reason why the medical examiner was never called at trial, and that was because the medical examiner would have told the truth on the stand. And the truth was that Becky was raped before she was murdered.

———

THE NEXT DAY, Regina was on a plane heading towards Kansas City. She really didn't like to fly. She always flew coach and for some reason, she always got stuck in the middle seat. She couldn't count the number of times she got stuck sitting next to some old coot, who apparently thought he had a chance with her and would talk to her the entire time they were on the flight. And when the flight was over, he would ask her what she was doing later on that day. Some of the time, Regina got the impression the men thought she was a working girl. She was inevitably insulted by that, because why would they think that about her? She didn't dress like a prostitute. And she tried to give every guy who hit on her on the plane the slip, but they usually never got the message.

On this particular flight, she got lucky. On her right was a teenage boy listening to something on his Beats headphones. The second the plane got into the air, he closed his eyes and leaned back in his chair. On her left was a young girl, probably about 15 years old. She was flipping through a magazine. She smiled at Regina and Regina got the impression she was shy. There was just something about her demeanor that made Regina imagine her sitting in her bedroom most nights, maybe reading, maybe watching something on the television, but not participating in online games, chat rooms, Tik Tok, Instagram, or anything like that.

Maybe that was just Regina projecting her imagination on this girl. At any rate, Regina could not help but think about how this girl was about the same age as the girls saved from Carl's ranch. Unlike those girls, this girl hopefully had her whole life ahead of her, trauma free. In Regina's mind, there would be no psychotherapists in her future, no waking up in a cold sweat every night because of having a nightmare about an old man forcing her to go down on his shriveled whiskey dick. She wouldn't have problems with intimacy, no self-esteem and insecurity problems. No sense of burning shame.

Regina knew enough about the root of her own problems to know that shame was at the core of all of it. It was shame that caused her to not want to get close to anybody. It was shame that caused her to not be able to sleep at night without having nightmares. It was shame that haunted her every waking moment of every day. She couldn't close her eyes without seeing them – the men who put money in her G string while she danced in front of them, copping a feel while they did it. The men who did unspeakable to things to her while she lay on the bed counting the popcorn dots on the ceiling. The men who would beat her, and, when she told Michael about them beating her, the only thing he could say was "I hope you got extra money from him, because you know I charge extra for that." And then, when she told him she didn't get extra money from these men, Michael would beat her as well.

As she looked at this young girl, projecting all her hopes for this girl's future, Regina felt a certain sense of satisfaction that she was helping Avery get Carl. She was helping these young girls through transitioning from the worst period of their lives. Yet, at the same time, she knew there were millions of other Carls out there. Millions of other Britneys. She couldn't not be happy knowing there were such monsters still in the world and an endless number of prey for them as well.

She wanted to tell this girl that she needed to keep her eyes open. The girl needed to know the signs of somebody who wanted to exploit her. She needed to not be too friendly with older men she didn't know. She needed to know that the world was a dangerous place and she needed to not be naïve. Regina would have told her all of this, except that she knew the girl would look at her like she was absolutely bonkers. And she would probably try to change her seat with somebody else. Regina knew that most girls like this girl next to her didn't see the world in quite the way she did. Most of them preferred to see the world as a place of good. Regina wished in her heart of hearts that she could have the same kind of outlook on life, but she just didn't. She was destined to be a Cassandra, warning people about what was to come and not being believed.

The plane touched down at KCI and Regina got off the plane with everybody else, not having said a word to this girl. And it was just as well. She was doubtful the girl would've ever listened to her anyway. She probably would've thought Regina was an absolute loon.

The first thing Regina did when she got off the plane was rent a car. Then after she rented a car, she got a room at the airport Hilton. That was the room Christian had reserved for her. She took her bags up to her room and then lay down on the bed, thinking about what she would be doing the next day. She only hoped she could be persuasive in getting the prosecutor to reopen the case.

———

THE NEXT DAY, she went to the Medical Examiner's Office to speak with the chief medical examiner. His name was Stellan Barner. He was a tall and lanky man, about 75, with white hair. A pair of glasses perched on the end of his long nose. He was dressed in a white lab coat and black pants.

He shook her hand. "Regina Baldwin? My name is Dr. Stellan Barner. I understand you wanted me to reopen the results of the autopsy for Becky Whitfield. I reviewed the file before you arrived, and I understand that you wanted me to analyze the DNA sample and compare it against a DNA sample on file for a Jurgen Williams. I took the liberty to do that, and the results were conclusive. The DNA that found inside Becky Whitfield matches that of Jurgen Williams."

Regina felt that was a foregone conclusion yet she was grateful all the same. "Now I know from the results of the autopsy that there was evidence she was raped before she was murdered. And what was the evidence that you saw for that?"

"Well, obviously, it's not easy to tell if a sexual encounter was consensual or not. But there were tears in the vagina consistent with forced penetration. There were also bruises on her abdomen and face that were consistent with being hit in the face and kicked in the abdomen. These signs were all consistent with forcible sexual assault. And if I would've been called to the stand in her case, during the first murder trial, I would have testified to just that. I was called to the stand on her retrial and that was my testimony."

Regina knew that to be true. She had carefully examined the entire file, and she saw that he had testified to exactly what he said to her in the retrial.

Regina spoke with the medical examiner for another half hour, just getting information together that she needed to get to present everything to the prosecutor's office. And then, after she was satisfied that she'd gotten the information she needed, she went drove down to the district attorney's office down the street.

———

"I'D LIKE to see Beth Ahern, please," Regina said politely to the receptionist at the prosecutor's office.

"What is this in regards to?"

"I need to talk to her about the Becky Whitfield case. I know she prosecuted the case for the retrial of Avery Collins. I need to talk to her about some new evidence I've obtained."

The receptionist took a look at her computer and then looked at Regina. "Looks like she has some free time at the moment. I'll give her a call and see if she's willing to speak with you. Just wait there."

Regina took a seat and flipped through some magazines while she waited for Beth to appear. In the magazine she read all about who was getting divorced, who was making up, who was having an affair with who. It was fascinating for her in a way, the trials and travails of the Hollywood stars, even though she knew that most of the stories in this particular tabloid were not accurate. To say the very least.

After she sat and waited for about 45 minutes, Beth finally appeared. "Regina Baldwin?" she said as she came into the lobby. Beth was a tall slim blonde, with curly hair, a long fine nose, and a very angular face. She had a genuine smile, which encouraged Regina. "I'm sorry to keep you waiting. I had to work on a motion for court today. But please, follow me to my office. I understand that you have some new evidence for me to look over in the Becky Whitfield case. It's been a closed case for a while, but we're always willing to take a look at these closed cases when something new comes up."

She followed Beth into her office and she sat down in a chair across from her desk. "Now," Beth began. "What is the new evidence you need to give to me?"

"I know who raped Becky before she died. There's some DNA on file for a guy by the name of Jurgen Williams. He's the son of Carl Williams. At the time of the trial and the retrial, there was no DNA on file for him. He recently got arrested for a DWI and DNA was taken from him at that time. Lo and behold, his DNA is a perfect match for the DNA found inside of Becky at the time she died."

Beth nodded. "I'll have to look into that."

Regina was unconvinced Beth would actually look into it. "There's also a lot of proof that Carl Williams was behind the railroading of Avery Collins in the first place. The prosecutor on Avery's case was also a regular guest at the Carl Williams compound. Follow the line from A to B to C, and you can see what happened. Carl Williams bribed Paul Sharpton, the prosecutor in the first Avery Collins trial, by promising him a lifetime membership to his sick child ranch. Paul moved out to San Diego right after Avery's trial was over. If Carl was bribing Paul to throw Avery under the bus, it stands to reason he was protecting somebody. Carl had an airtight alibi for the crime. So he wasn't the one who did it. Anyhow, I just think the hard evidence of the DNA, combined with the circumstantial evidence about Paul ending up in San Diego, and being a part of Carl's client list almost immediately after the trial, tells you everything you need to know."

Beth still looked unconvinced. "I know what you're saying. But this case is closed and I have an entire roster of active cases I need to work on."

Regina could not believe what she was hearing. "So what are you saying? Jurgen Williams is out there and could be hurting girls and women even as we speak. And he still has his daddy to protect him. I mean, I know his daddy is over in Europe right now because he's too chicken to face the people over here who hate his guts and want to tear him limb from limb, but you know he still is protecting that guy. That means he'll continue to get away with doing what he's doing."

Beth took a deep breath, stood up and closed the door. "I'm not going to lie to you," she said as she sat back down. "I know what you're saying. Believe me, I get it. But I take my orders from the higher-ups, and the higher ups have explicitly told us assistant district attorneys that we are not to file any cases that involve Carl Williams. I don't really know why. I've heard rumors about some blackmail schemes going on with some of the senior attorneys in this office. I don't really know. All I know is that if I decided to file a case against this guy, I would be out of a job. Why do you think Avery Collins got railroaded in the first place? I'll tell you why. It wasn't that Paul was being bribed by Carl. The fact that Paul went out to San Diego and was accepted into the Carl Williams' world was a bonus for him, but that wasn't why he did what he did with your friend. No. What happened with your friend was an order from people much higher than Paul."

Regina closed her eyes. "I don't understand. You do know Carl isn't being protected by the Ivanov family anymore, don't you? That's the why Carl's on the lam even as we speak. Not only that, but the cat's out of the bag with that guy. Everybody knows what he did with those kids. There's no secret to keep anymore. Come on, you cannot let this guy still be out on the streets, doing what he's doing with these girls."

Beth just shook her head. "Believe me, I've had more fights about this very topic than you care to know. To tell the truth, I was absolutely relieved that Avery got a new trial. And I was relieved I was prosecuting it. I didn't try very hard to win that case, believe me. A hundred-year-old attorney who is deaf, dumb, and blind could have won that case for Avery. That was because I knew she was innocent. And that didn't go well with the higher ups at all. They wanted me to be aggressive in trying to win that case, because they needed her to stay in prison for Becky's murder. They knew that if Avery was found not guilty, they were going to be pressured to find Becky's real killer. Avery was found not guilty and this office has been pressured. But nothing has happened on that case and nothing ever will. I'm sorry. I wish I could tell you something different, but I like my job and I'm very good at it. If I filed charges against Jurgen Williams, I'll be out on the street in no time."

"This is a hill to die on," Regina said. "If there is any hill to die on, it's this one. Come on, have a little backbone. Just think how you'll feel when this guy does it again. You know he's going to. He might've already. Who knows? He might be Ted Bundy in disguise. He might've left a whole trail of bodies. You have a chance to put this guy behind bars. Any jury will convict on these facts. All you got to do is file the charges."

"I'm sorry, but the answer is no."

Regina just shook her head. She could not believe what she was hearing. She was serving this guy up on a silver platter and they weren't going to do a thing about it.

For once in her life, she felt speechless. Helpless. Was there really nothing that could be done to bring this guy to justice? She knew Avery was working on the civil case, but she was in jail at the moment, and it seemed that this Jonathan Augusto person wouldn't just play hardball, he would play down and dirty.

And now this.

"I guess there's nothing more to say," I said. "But the next time this guy does it, I'm going to let you know about it. And you know there will be a next time. There always is. A guy like that doesn't just start out violent and then change his ways. Especially when he's being protected by everybody. Have a nice life."

Regina turned to walk out the door, but Beth stood up. "Regina. Wait. Please."

Regina turned around. Her arms were folded in front of her in a defensive posture. "Yes. What do you want?"

Beth looked around the room as if she was thinking somebody would hear her. "Listen, you're an investigator. You don't happen to have access to a reporter or anyone like that, do you? Do you know anybody media savvy who might want a story?"

"As a matter of fact, I know somebody like that. His name is Ari Romo and he's a reporter with the New York *Times.* He broke the story about Carl Williams and his ring. Why?"

Beth leaned forward and talked to Regina in a quiet

voice. It was such a quiet voice that Regina could hardly hear her. "There's a story your friend might be interested in. Tell him he needs to look into the death of a girl by the name of Allegra Chianti. Five years old, hit-and-run. Nobody ever found the culprit. There's a story there. That's all I'm going to say."

Regina suddenly understood. She understood very well. Something told her somebody high up in the prosecutor's office was responsible for the death of that little girl, or, more likely, had a kid responsible for the death of that little girl. "On it. Thanks."

Regina left the office and knew what she had to do. If she ever wanted there to be a kibosh on the apparent office-wide ban on prosecuting anybody associated with Carl Williams, she would have to figure out that story and threaten to go public with it. Maybe then, and only then, could she have the leverage to finally get this bastard the justice he so sorely needed.

Chapter Twenty-Five

CHRISTIAN FINALLY GOT me out of jail sometime after midnight. By that time, I was freezing, starving and had a headache that had been beating down for the past five hours. To say that I wasn't in a good mood was understating the matter.

"I assume I'm taking you home, right?" Christian asked.

"God yes. All I want to do is go home and get into my king-size bed, with my two girls, and sleep for like 100 hours. But we're also going to have to figure out how to try this case. We're going up against somebody who will use anything and everything to try to prevent us from making headway. I think it's time for you to do a little hacking and see if we can come up with something to fight fire with fire with this guy. And if it comes right down to it, I think it's time for us to do some dirty tricks of our own. We gotta show this guy we will not to be intimidated."

"That's true, but in the meantime, you got a cocaine possession case to worry about. You could lose your bar license if you get convicted for that. If that happens, you'll be no good for anybody."

"Leave that to me."

THAT WEEK, I got the surprise of my life. I got a letter in the mail from the prosecutor's office explaining that they wouldn't prosecute me for the cocaine possession charge.

Huh. I filed the letter away, but I was curious as to what happened.

I soon found out.

"So, what did you think of my opening shot?" Jonathan Augusto's booming voice was on the other line. "Believe me, that's just a taste."

"I suppose you also got the prosecutors to drop the charges against me, didn't you?"

"Damn right. I wanted to show you exactly how much power I have over them. I say jump, they say how high. It's all just a show, kabuki. And, trust me, next time it won't be so minor. Don't forget that I've been responsible for planting dead hookers in people's beds. This isn't my first rodeo."

"Just like you sent your opening shot, you just wait for mine. I'm not some shrinking violet. I've been to prison. I'm not scared of anything. And that includes you and your dirty tricks," I said.

He just started to laugh. "Okay I'll be looking for your shot. Let's see if you can give as good as you get. My assumption is that you'll be dismissing this case with prejudice, I repeat with prejudice, by the end of the week."

I hung up the phone and knew this was a fight I couldn't back down from. There was something about being threatened by people who apparently didn't play the game in any kind of an ethical way, to say the very least, that got my back up. I was so tired of everybody in this case throwing their muscle around. I knew why they were. The only way to protect pedophiles such as Carl would be to play dirty. If people weren't willing to play dirty, Carl would've been in prison a long time ago. He certainly would not be making millions upon millions of dollars off of wealthy child rapists if he didn't have a whole slew of people willing to do anything and everything to make sure he continued his dirty ways.

I would have to plan my own salvo to him.

I went down the hall to Christian's office. "You finding anything on Jonathan yet?" I asked him.

He shook his head. "No. I haven't. I've been hacking his system and so far I haven't been able to find anything incriminating against him. Even his bank accounts seem to be pretty kosh. I've seen no evidence of any kind of criminal activity so far."

"Well that doesn't really matter, does it?" I asked rhetorically. "I mean, this guy apparently has prosecutors in his pocket just like Carl did. Even if there was something criminal he's up to, chances are no one's gonna do anything about it. We just have to figure something out to humiliate him publicly. Or threaten to humiliate him publicly, so he'll back the hell off and let me try this case. All I want is try to win this case fair and square. I don't want to humiliate him into throwing it. I just want him to stop with his dirty tricks."

"So what are you thinking about?"

"We need Ari Romo on this. We need to do something to get Ari to threaten to file a story about it. This guy's a celebrity attorney. He's also a celebrity fixer. We need to figure out his soft spot, his Achilles' heel, and poke it. We need to do the equivalent of a dead hooker in his bed and then threaten him with publicity about it. As you know, he's not afraid of the legal system. But he might be afraid of a front page story in the New York *Times* about it."

Christian smiled. "What about an actual dead hooker in the bed? It worked in *Godfather Part Two.*"

"Where are we going to get a dead hooker?" I asked. "Besides, there's not much we can do even with a dead hooker. Nobody's going to prosecute him for anything, especially not a dead hooker, because who really cares about them, right? I'm being facetious, of course. I care about dead hookers, so do you, so does everybody with a heart. But I'm just saying the prosecutor's office would not prosecute him for something like that. And even if we tried to use a dead hooker as bad publicity, that wouldn't work, either. He would just revel in it. He's the kind of guy that believes any publicity is good publicity, unless it's something that gets at his Achilles heel. We don't really know what that is yet."

"So I guess a horse's head is out as well, huh?" he said, referring to the scene in the first *Godfather* where the movie producer woke up with the head of his dead race horse in his bed.

"That's what I'm saying. There has to be something else. Something we can really get this guy on. We need all hands on deck for this. Let's meet at my condo this evening. Aidan will be home tonight, I'll invite Regina, we'll order in, and we can brainstorm this. Two heads are better than one, and four heads are better than two."

"Where is Regina, anyhow?"

"She's working the Kansas City angle. Last I heard, she was talking to the prosecutor about reopening the Becky Whitfield murder case. She was going to talk to the medical examiner and see if the DNA found inside Becky matched the DNA for that Jurgen guy. If it did, hopefully that would give the prosecutor enough information to pursue charges."

Christian got up and went back to his office. He had a motion he was working on for a court appearance at 1:30. I looked at the clock and wondered myself how Regina was doing. I hadn't heard from her since I got out of jail.

I had a sinking feeling there was something wrong.

I just didn't know exactly what.

Chapter Twenty-Six

REGINA

REGINA SPENT the next three days turning over every single rock she could investigating the Allegra Chianti hit-and-run case. Little Allegra was only five years old when she was struck by a motorcycle going 70 mph in a 25 mph school zone. Regina started with the police report and spoke with every witness she could possibly speak with. She was beginning to think this was another dead end when she decided to look a little deeper.

She called Christian and asked him to hack into the files of the Kansas City Police Department. She wanted to see if there was anything buried in the archives about this case.

Ten minutes later, she got her answer. "There was an arrest made. A Jerry Astin was brought in for questioning. He was also arrested. Turns out his bike had damage consistent with having hit a child, he was wearing the same clothing that witnesses said the guy on the bike was wearing, and he was three sheets to the wind. He blew .25. The blood test came back that he was also high on cocaine. And, the kicker is, he confessed."

"Jerry Astin, who is he?" Regina would have to look into this Jerry Astin guy. She would also have to look into exactly why this case was buried and what it had to do with the Becky Whitfield case.

"I don't know. That's up to you. Try to figure out who that guy is, who might've been able to bury it, and who might've been able to use it. Good luck."

Regina got on the computer and looked for some records on this Jerry Astin kid. She found out he was the son of a guy by the name of Ronald Astin. At the time the Becky Whitfield case was working its way through the court system, this Jerry Astin kid apparently was racking up DWIs like they were going out of style. Every single one of them, however, got dismissed.

When Regina started looking into Ron Astin's background, she figured out why every one of Jerry's charges got dismissed. Ron Astin was a state senator and was in charge of the committee that funded the Jackson County prosecutor's office. That told Regina everything she needed to know. She put two and two together and figured that every time his shady kid got arrested for yet another DWI, this Ron Astin guy probably threatened the prosecutor's office with a choke of funding unless they declined to prosecute him.

What Regina didn't know was how Ron Astin was associated with Becky Whitfield's case. He evidently was. But how?

Some additional digging led Regina to the answer. Apparently, in 2006, Carl Williams was in line to buy the Kansas City *Star*. The *Star* is the paper of record in Kansas City. When Regina went to the archives of the articles that didn't make it to print, with the help of Christian, who hacked the Kansas City *Star* archives the same way he hacked the KCPD arrest archives, she saw a major article was killed. This was an article that threatened to expose Jerry Astin for the kid he was. It also threatened to expose all the coverups Ron was responsible for with regards to his kid. A major story was going to be published after Jerry Astin had confessed to having killed Allegra Chianti, but the story was killed right after Carl Williams apparently endowed the newspaper with a $1 million donation.

Regina got the picture. The way she saw it, Jürgen Williams was probably being looked at for the murder of Becky Whitfield back in the fall of 2006. The case might've even been referred to the prosecutor's office from the KCPD. Carl knew exactly how to make sure the Jackson County prosecutor's office didn't prosecute his son. She could imagine that what happened was that Carl had a talk with Ron Astin and informed him that unless he leaned on the prosecutors not to prosecute his son, he would buy the Kansas City *Star* and blare front-page headlines about Jerry Astin having confessed to killing a five-year-old girl while drunk off his ass and then leaving the scene. For good measure, he might've even threatened Ron by showing him a rough copy of the story going to print.

And then, once the Jackson County prosecutor's office stopped looking at Jurgen, and filed charges against Avery, Carl gave millions of dollars to the paper not to run the Jerry Astin story. Regina saw in the evidence an unholy alliance between Carl Williams, Ron Astin, and the prosecutor's office. Ron made the prosecutor's office dance to his tune, because he was a powerful state senator who had the power to cut off funding to the Jackson County's prosecutor's office if he wanted to.

So, it was possible that Paul Sharpton was just a pawn in all of this game-playing after all. Paul might've been reinforced by Carl, in that Carl might've promised him membership to his club in exchange for doing all he could to hide the ball from the court in Avery's case. But the corruption went much higher than Regina thought possible.

Once she told Avery what she found out, Avery wouldn't be happy. After all, Avery was responsible for that guy's suicide. What if Paul was just a pawn, being forced into doing what he did by people higher up on the food chain than him?

Then again, he was responsible for the San Diego prosecutor's office not prosecuting Carl. So maybe he got his just desserts after all. Not to mention the fact that he was a perv doing pervy things. All Avery was doing was trying to force him into doing the right thing and he decided he was better off dead. That was his choice.

At any rate, when she discovered Ron Astin had ambitions for higher office, specifically that he was in the race for the United States Senate, she saw her opening.

She would have to pay a visit to Ron. And she would have to call Ari, tell him what she needed, and hope that perhaps he would do her a little favor in this case.

———

ARI WAS unable to fly out to Kansas City for a couple of days, so Regina had to make a decision. She knew Avery needed her back in San Diego. Avery was apparently cooking up an idea about how to put Jonathan Augusto into check. She needed her input and needed her connections to make all that happen.

So she decided to fly back to San Diego for a couple of days, and then meet Ari back in Kansas City when he could make it. She had the perfect plan to make Ron Astin finally cut Carl Williams loose. Regina knew that circumstances with Carl had changed since 2006. He was no longer the powerful wealthy guy he was. He was still wealthy but was currently living in Sweden and wasn't being protected by organized crime anymore. Knowing all that, Regina had a pretty good idea that if she threatened Ron with a major story in the New York *Times* about all the cover-up shenanigans that went on involving his son over the years, Ron would change his tune on the stranglehold he had with the prosecutor's office. He was desperately trying to avoid publicity back in the day and maybe he was still afraid that Carl would expose him.

All she had to do was make him more afraid that *she* would expose him. She would put that guy into a box and make him do the right thing.

In the meantime, however, she had to help Avery.

Chapter Twenty-Seven

AVERY

REGINA FLEW BACK to San Diego and I finally was able to get my brainstorming session underway. I was starting to come up with a small kernel of an idea on how to hit back at Jonathan Augusto. This idea was just that at the moment. An idea.

Regina, Christian, Aidan and I met at my condo that evening. I ordered Chinese takeout, I got some bottles of wine ready, and all of us gathered around my dining room table that evening to enjoy some Chinese food and wine and talk about how we were going to get Jonathan.

"Christian has hacked Jonathan's financials and he has found nothing amiss," I said. "Also, apparently, Jonathan has not actually downloaded child porn onto his computer. And even if he did, I don't think that would be the magic bullet to make him back off. Nobody's gonna prosecute him for anything. Like Carl, he just knows too much dirt on everybody in town. As for any kind of bad publicity, I don't think he cares. Nobody thinks he's an angel. In fact, his clients hire him because he's not an angel. They expect him to be a bad boy."

"What if we catch him in bed with some dude?" Aidan wanted to know.

"Who cares? Besides, the attorney he has apparently modeled himself after, Roy Cohn, was a homosexual who died of AIDS. Who knows? Jonathan might see a picture of him with some guy to be a badge of honor. So I don't think that setting him up with a rent boy, and then trying to take pictures of him, will do it," I said.

"What if he's involved with the mob?" Christian asked.

"I don't know. He probably *is* involved with the mob," I said.

Regina was nodding. "Well, there's one thing I found out about this Jonathan guy, and it's that he likes to gamble. In Vegas, he owes millions of dollars to a casino that's owned by a Ukrainian gangster by the name of Dmytro Antonich. Dude's got a marker there for $10 million. What if we could get Dmytro to call in that marker? We don't know much about Jonathan, but I don't think he's that liquid. I think he would have a tough time trying to pay the $10 million in a short period of time."

"That's a great idea, but how will we get Dmytro to call in the marker?" I asked. "Or, rather, threaten to call in the marker. That's the most important thing. If he calls in the marker, it won't do any good. It's the threat of doing that that would make Jonathan back the hell off."

"Okay. This is how you do it."

And Regina gave me a step-by-step instruction on how I would hopefully get Dmytro influenced enough that he would call in the marker or threaten that.

Chapter Twenty-Eight

THE NEXT DAY, I found myself heading back to Bakersfield, California, to go to the medium security prison there. Regina told me I was to talk to a guy by the name of Harrison Baker. As she explained it, Harrison Baker was part of the Armenian mob, and his clan, the Aslanian clan, worked with mobsters from Russia and Ukraine. Harrison was serving time as a fall guy, but Regina said that, as the hacker for the Aslanian clan, he knew where the bodies were buried. Literally. He was the one who apparently got Yuri Ivanov to drop his partnership with Carl. And there was a good chance he could talk to Dmytro about threatening to call in the Vegas marker for Jonathan.

So I went to the pod where Harrison Baker was staying. He came out about half-hour after I got there and he smiled when he looked at me. "Let me guess. You're a friend of Regina's, right?"

I nodded. "Yes. My name is Avery Collins, and –"

At that, Harrison embraced me in a spontaneous hug. "My daughter, Emma, came to see me. She visited for two hours. And she told me everything she was doing with Carl Williams. She also told me she was living in a group home with the other girls in North Park. She said the person who arranged for that group home was a gal by the name of Avery Collins. You. She said you and Regina were like her guardian angels or something. I'm not going to lie, she's pretty messed up. She's working with a therapist, and everything, over at that group home. But she's back in school and my bitch wife will lose that La Jolla home. She don't have my daughter working no more to pay that mortgage so she's going to be going bye-bye. Anyhow, Avery, I can't tell you how glad I am to meet you."

I felt relieved. "I'm so glad. The reason I'm here is not just to see you and see how you're doing. I'm curious about that. How are you?"

"Good. I'm getting out of here in 10 months. There's not much to do around here but it's not so bad. I mean, I would love to go to a minimum security place, places where there's rock concerts and pool tables, but it is what it is. What can I do for you?"

"Regina tells me you have a lot of information on a lot of different mobsters around town, and that you might be able to help me with something. There is a mobster, a Ukrainian mobster, by the name of Dmytro Antonich. He operates out of San Diego, but he also owns a string of casinos in Vegas. Do you know any thing about him?"

"Oh yeah. I know that guy. Everybody knows that guy. At least anybody associated with the Eastern European clans know who he is. Why do you ask?"

"And I understand you have some pretty high-up protection on your life, isn't that right?"

"Of course. Nobody's going to hit me, not unless somebody wants to create a war. I've got hacking skills that are second to none. In fact, I've been in demand with a lot of high politicians in the area. National politicians who want me to hack and find dirt on their opponents. Trust me, I'm safe. So what do you want me to do?"

"I want you to use your influence with Dmytro to call in a marker for a guy by the name of Jonathan Augusto. Actually, I just want Dmytro to threaten it. I don't want him to actually call it in, I just want him to threaten to do so. Have him tell Jonathan that the only way he won't call in that marker is if he agrees to back off me. Jonathan is making it impossible for me to properly try a civil case I have against Carl. He's already had me put in jail for something I didn't do. He planted drugs in my car and then got an informant to call the police. I was arrested and spent almost a whole day in jail. And then, just to show me he could do it, he had the prosecutors dismiss the charges against me. All I want is a fair fight. The only way I'm going to get a fair fight is if Jonathan agrees to play fair. The only way he's going to agree to play fair is if something is being held over his head, like the possibility of being killed because he can't pay a $10 million marker. Could you do that for me?"

"You got it. You're suing Carl?"

"Yeah. I think that's the only way I can get him. The only way that anybody's going to get him is in a civil court. Nobody's willing to prosecute him, still."

"Then you got it. I'll do anything to help that bastard come to justice. After what he did to my daughter, I'd like to kill him myself. But I know he's got some place in Sweden where he's hiding out. And I still got my marching orders that no one is to lay a glove on him, criminally anyway, for reasons I don't understand. I only know the guy's got dirt on everybody in town. So I know what you're saying, he prob-

Chapter Twenty-Nine

REGINA

REGINA WENT TO JEFFERSON CITY, Missouri, to confront Ron Astin, with Ari in tow. When they got to Jefferson City, Ari made a face. Regina knew what he was thinking. Jeff City wasn't exactly the most urbane capitol city in the entire world, to say the very least. The buildings outside the window were old and worn and there just seemed to be a sense of despair that permeated the air in this town.

Yet the capitol building, where Regina and Ari were headed, was beautiful. It was there that she fell in love with the art of Thomas Hart Benton. The Benton mural in the House Lounge was the most amazing thing she'd ever seen. The rotunda had its own works of art, with women walking around with baskets of fruits on their heads and lots of blues and oranges. Visiting this capitol was one of the few happy memories she had of her childhood.

They would ambush this guy. Regina managed to get a copy of Ron's schedule and saw he had an opening at 2:30. She made an arrangement with his chief of staff to see him, by calling the chief of staff and lying about who she was. She explained that her name was Angela Queensland and was a lobbyist for the poultry industry and needed to talk to Ron about some pending legislation. That was the only way she could get in to talk to him. She felt badly to be lying like that, until she thought about what this guy was up to, then felt that anything that happened to him was probably deserved.

They got to the capitol building and found Ron's office suite. Regina explained to the receptionist who she was, and, within 15 minutes, she and Ron were heading back to Ron's office.

"Hello," Ron said as Regina and Ari sat down in chairs in front of his enormous desk. "What can I do for the two of you?"

Ron's decor seemed to favor the gaudy - his curtains were gold, as were his walls, which were papered in gold lamé. Ron himself seemed like a tacky kind of guy, really - his suit didn't fit him well, and his hair was done in an extremely obvious combover. The guy was around 30 lbs overweight and probably was less than 5'5". His legs were tiny and spindly, his gut was huge and he had sizeable man boobs.

"I'm not going to beat around the bush, here," Regina said. "My name isn't really Angela Queensland. It's Regina Baldwin. I'm a private investigator. This is Ari Romo. He's a reporter for the New York *Times*. He's going to file a story in the New York *Times* about your son, Jerry, and about his DWIs and his confession to killing a five-year-old girl while shit-faced and going 75 MPH on his bike through a residential neighborhood. His story will also talk about all the coverups going on in the Jackson County prosecutor's office, because you led the appropriations committee that funded the office and you threatened to choke off funds for the office unless they turned a blind eye to your son's f-ups. I mean, he killed a young girl. A five-year-old girl who was chasing after a ball when your son came barreling down the street, too blind drunk to see her."

Ron's face, which had a bit of an orange tint, with white around his eyes, as he apparently self-tanned with goggles on, suddenly got very pale. His rheumy blue eyes - he seemed to share his son's love of the drink, judging by how bloodshot his eyes were - darted from Regina to Ari and back again. "What are you talking about?"

"Don't play dumb," Regina said. "I have all the evidence I need to expose exactly what happened. I have a copy of the police report, all the police reports for all of Jerry's DWIs, and I have circumstantial evidence that you threatened to choke off the funding to the Jackson County prosecutor's office unless they didn't pursue charges against your son for anything at all. I admit, we're still investigating and interviewing witnesses, but just the fact that your son had what, 10 DWIs in the span of two years, and no prosecutions, is proof enough that a major shakedown was happening in that office."

Ron knew that he was caught. Regina could see that by looking at his face. She raised an eyebrow at him and folded her arms.

"What do you want?" he asked. "You want something. I know you do. If you didn't, you would've just written the story and been done with it. Now what do you want?"

"I want you to take off the kibosh on prosecuting anybody associated with Carl Williams for the murder of Becky Whitfield. I have found evidence that Jurgen Williams, Carl's son, was behind the murder of Becky. The prosecutor's office won't do anything about it because you've threatened them not to. You need to take off the stranglehold you have over there and allow a prosecution to go forward. That's what I want."

He shook his head. "I can't do that. I have an agreement with Carl. If I go back on that, I-"

"You what?" Regina demanded. "What? Listen, Carl is in Sweden. He's been run out of this country on a rail. He's not in with the mob anymore. You're not going to end up floating in the Mississippi River if you cross him. On the other hand, if you don't do what I ask, Ari will go public with the story. In fact, he's going to go public with the story about Jerry's crimes, no matter what. The public has a right to know. The public might forgive you, eventually, because it was so long ago. But if Ari writes a story that you're *currently* corrupt and *currently* carrying water for a child rapist and murderer, well, you'll be lucky to be elected dog-catcher. And you'll be in prison yourself."

Ron narrowed his eyes and got a bottle of whiskey out of a drawer. He put it to his lips and took a large swig of it and then wiped his mouth with the back of his hand. "You go forward with that story about my son, and I will go to the joint, that's for sure."

"No you won't. The statute of limitations has run on all your extortion crimes. But if you *keep* extorting the Jackson County prosecutor's office and *keep* them from filing charges against Jurgen, then, yes, your ass will be in a prison cell in no time."

"But my son, he's going to be prosecuted for killing that little girl."

"Cry me a river. That girl is dead because your son was riding his motorcycle through a residential neighborhood, going 75 miles per hour while shit-faced. He needs to be held to account."

Ron took another large swig of his whiskey. He knew he was screwed. So was his son. There was nothing that could be done.

"I'll call my guy at the prosecutor's office today," he said. "And they will be allowed to prosecute that Jurgen person." He was a defeated man. So was his son. Regina couldn't feel sorry for either of them. The father enabled the son, who apparently never grew up. Regina found out that Jerry Astin continued to be a monster, probably because he was allowed to be one when he was young. He was currently 38 years old and had had several restraining orders on him over the years. He was a rich guy and Regina knew he would buy his his way out of trouble, as rich guys always do.

But at least he would face charges.

———

REGINA WENT BACK to see Beth Ahern two days later. Beth smiled at Regina when she showed up in her office. "I've looked at the evidence against Jurgen and I'm recommending charges. He's been arrested in San Diego and is *en route* to Missouri for extradition as we speak. I hope there will finally be justice for Becky Whitfield. God, I hope that poor girl can finally get justice."

"Me too," Regina said, thinking about Avery. "Justice for Becky and for Avery."

Chapter Thirty

I GOT the phone call from Regina, telling me that, at long last, somebody would stand trial for the murder of Becky all those years ago. While I didn't necessarily think Jurgen would be convicted, because he had the money to get the best justice money could buy, I was happy that he was going through the motions of a criminal trial.

That made me happy.

What also made me happy was that the case against Carl was going forward. The class was certified, discovery was exchanged, and I had done several depositions of the people around the compound when those young girls were being raped. They all seemed apprehensive about talking to me. I had to reassure all of them that they would not be prosecuted, which was true. The prosecutor told me they didn't plan to pursue any of the ancillary people and I told each of them that they were safe to speak with me. And they did. In deposition after deposition, I heard the same types of stories.

The entire thing made me sick, but I knew my deposition of Carl would shed a lot of light on exactly what happened. I had a long list of questions for him.

To tell the truth, I didn't want to try this case. The girls were doing relatively well in the group home I created for them. A lot of them were still suffering from PTSD, but I made sure that all the girls got intense therapy, at least the ones who were still suffering the most, and they all were in school. And they all had each other. That was important. They were around others who knew what they were going through. They had each other to lean on.

I didn't want to drag them through the pain of a trial. So, if there was any way to have persuaded this guy to give me the money I was looking for, without there being a trial, I would do it. As it was, I was trying to figure out a way to try the case without calling any of the girls to the stand. I knew that was an option. There were enough witnesses to what was going on that I probably could do it without them being re-victimized on the stand. And with Jonathan being cowed by the threat of the Ukrainian gangster killing him for not paying his marker, I knew there was a good chance I could win the case without a single girl taking the stand.

So I took Carl's deposition. It took 8 hours and he lied all the way through it. He somehow tried to make it seem like he didn't do a thing wrong, and that when he hired those girls, he thought they were all of age because they all had fake IDs. Then he tried to say that the parties weren't sex parties, they were just regular parties. When those men disappeared with those girls, all of whom were 21, according to him, they weren't going to places to have sex. They were just going places to make out. No sex ever happened on his grounds, none at all. And certainly nobody underaged appeared at these parties, at least none that he knew of. He was shocked, shocked, that these hussies all gave him fake IDs. How was he to know they were lying?

He dared me to prove that any sex happened on his grounds during these parties.

I would do exactly that.

I knew he wouldn't appear for trial and that was fine. No way would he ever set foot on United States soil, because the pressure was high for the prosecutor's office to throw the book at him. I knew the prosecutors hoped he would never return to this country because they didn't want to deal with it.

Nevertheless, I would show this deposition to the jury and they were going to know how much of a liar and gaslighter Carl was.

Chapter Thirty-One

AS IT TURNED OUT, I didn't settle the case. I decided to talk to the girls and ask all of them if they were okay with taking the stand, and I knew that I needed to find a few girls who might have been mentally okay with testifying.

Naomi King stood up and told me that she wanted to testify. Naomi was a beautiful black girl, with cheekbones that could cut glass, big brown eyes framed by the thickest eyelashes I had ever seen, and dimples. She had natural hair that fell around her face with large curls. She was a skinny girl, although she had strong legs and curvy hips.

"Ms. Avery, if you need somebody to get up there and tell what happened to us girls, I'll do it. I want to do it."

Three other girls concurred. One was named Angela Todd. She was a tall red-head, willowy and statuesque with natural curls, light green eyes and broad shoulders. The second girl was Dakota Murphy. She was a natural brunette but had taken to streaking her hair with midnight blue. Like everybody else in the house, she was gorgeous, with dark eyes, a straight Roman nose, perfect teeth and full lips. She easily could have walked the runway. The third girl was Cameron Hayes. A skinny blonde, Cameron was only 15, the youngest of the group who volunteered to take the stand, as the other three girls were 17. But she was probably one of the self-possessed of all the girls in the house.

They all gave similar reasons for wanting to testify. "We need to make the case against the guy as strong as we can," Angela informed me. "I've been talking a lot to that shrink and I realize that what he did to us wasn't just wrong, but criminal. Us girls are going to go through this horrible trauma for the rest of our lives."

"And we need to get some cash for what we went through," Dakota said bluntly. "Listen, some of the girls in this house won't be able to get over what happened. They might not ever be able to work a job. That's how bad they're traumatized. They're going to need money and if the only way they're going to get it is that the four of us take the stand, then that's what we'll do."

Cameron chimed in. "I agree, Ms. Collins," she said. "Somebody needs to take this guy down. What he did to us, he needs to pay for it."

Naomi simply said she was looking forward to taking the stand. "I want to look that guy in the eye and tell him exactly what I think about him. I think my therapist calls it closure."

So I got my core group of girls. I prepared them for what they were going to experience on the stand. "You're going to get cross-examined by a guy who has it in his bones to be a ruthless jerk," I said.

"I know," Cameron said, with a roll of her eyes. "I watch *CSI*. And *Law and Order*. I know all about cross-examinations. I'm ready for it."

Still, even though the girls all told me they were prepared, I spent days and days preparing them anyhow.

I also managed to certify their therapists as both an expert witness on the effects of child sexual molestation and rape, as well as a witness about the mental trauma the girls were experiencing because of Carl's sickness.

I was ready for trial. Christian would second-chair me and I felt like it was the dynamic duo together again. We did so well with the Esme Gutierrez case and I was happy the two of us could team up again. We prepared for trial by staying at the North Park house with the girls so Christian could prepare them for trial while I spread out the evidence on a table in the sunroom and went over everything I possibly could.

Chapter Thirty-Two

December 16 – The First Day of Trial

WHEN I GOT to the courthouse on the first day of the trial, ready to pick my jury, I knew I would win. It was just a matter of how much we would be awarded. I decided that, come what may, I would give most of the money to the girls. They deserved it. Besides, I had more than enough money. I was never the girl who needed a lot of money. I only just ever wanted to be comfortable. And my $10 million settlement with the state of Missouri was stretching very far.

Then again, I didn't know what the girls would do with all that money. Most of them didn't really have a family to help them manage their finances. Since many of the girls were minors, the state of California would have a guardian *ad litem* appointed to them. A guardian *ad litem* was basically an attorney who decided what was the best interest of the child. Most likely, any money they received from this lawsuit would go into trust for them, or a structured settlement, where the minor would get a certain amount each month from the settlement, at least until they turned 21.

So I knew that any amount of money they received would be safe for them, in that they couldn't just spend it all wildly. And some of the girls who I managed to bring into the class were adults now. They could spend the money however they chose.

Yet, I also knew that most of these girls were unsophisticated, didn't have very good role models, and I was concerned for them. If we won big in court, they would be instant millionaires. How would they handle that?

Yet I knew that was the least of everybody's problem. We all just had to get through the next week or so.

And that was making me very, very nervous.

Chapter Thirty-Three

I WAS SURPRISED to see a crowd of people standing out in front of the courthouse when I arrived for trial, but maybe I shouldn't have been. This case was drawing a considerable amount of attention, due to the notoriety of Carl and his pedophilia ring. Because Carl was a billionaire, and his clientele was made up of the elite, this case was drawing its fair share of national attention as well. There was a lot of pressure on the prosecutors here to file charges against Carl, and they did, but only because there was so much pressure on them to do so. But the prosecutors didn't do anything to extradite Carl from Sweden and I knew that Carl wouldn't come back anytime soon. That was why I took his video-taped deposition. I knew the guy wouldn't be setting foot on United States soil anytime soon, and I couldn't force him to. He knew that, because of all the pressure and notoriety, he'd be arrested the second he came to this country.

As it was, there were multiple defamation cases going on, filed by the men whose names were published in the New York *Times* after Carl voluntarily broke up his ring.

They were probably going to win, too, because everybody was circling the wagons and everybody was clamming up about exactly who were at these parties. Again, this was predictable. I wasn't really concerning myself with all of that, though. While I didn't like that these wealthy and powerful men were suing for defamation, when they all clearly were regulars at Carl's parties, their cases were not my focus.

This one was.

A bunch of people standing in the crowd recognized me as being the attorney for the girls, and several of them came up to me.

"You're doing God's work," one lady said to me, tears in her eyes. "I've been reading about you. You saved those girls."

Other women came up and said similar things.

"I was abused when I was young, and I would have loved to have you on my side."

"I've been praying for you and the girls since I found out this happened."

"That guy should be burned alive. He's too cowardly to come here and face the music and I hope you cut his nuts off in court."

And so on.

I felt embarrassed by all the attention. I was used to people hating me, because, usually I was defending some guy or girl who everybody assumed was a scumbag, and I'd gotten my share of death threats over the years because of it. But I knew my role in this case would get me nothing but praise, and too much praise always embarrassed me. I didn't know why, but I always have had a hard time accepting too many compliments.

I got into the courthouse and took a deep breath as I

took the express elevator to the 13th Floor. I tried not to feel like I was unlucky, even though the courtroom was on the 13th floor. Maybe things were going to be unlucky for Jonathan and Carl, but not for me.

Still, I couldn't quite calm my frayed nerves.

When I got into the courtroom, Jonathan was there. He didn't have a second-chair. His enormous girth was straining at the buttons on his shirt. He didn't yet have on a jacket and I could see sweat stains on his armpits. He was wearing cowboy boots and grey flannel pants, and his face was really red and blotchy. I wondered if he would have a heart attack in front of the jury because he was breathing heavily and sweating so much. Then again, he was really overweight, so maybe sweating and breathing heavily were typical for him.

I went over to him and I could smell stale whiskey on his breath. I wondered how stale the whiskey was. Was it from the night before or was it from that morning?

He brought out a water bottle. I could smell that it was pure vodka, and I had my answer.

This will be interesting.

"You ready for this?" I asked him.

"Lady, you don't know how ready I am for this," he said. "I can't wait for you to put on your evidence. I'll be cross examining all your lying bitches on the stand and I can't wait for that."

I rolled my eyes. So, that was how he was going to play it. He was going to show my traumatized plaintiffs were "lying bitches."

Yeah, that would go over well.

Christian arrived next, and, after everybody was assembled in the courtroom, Judge Foster came on the bench.

"We'll be calling in the jury pool soon, but, for now, I'd

like to entertain any motions that the counselors might have. Now, Ms. Collins, do you have any motions for the court to entertain?"

"No, your honor," I said. "But I reserve the right to file a motion *in limine* at a later date."

"Mr. Augusto?" he asked Jonathan.

"Yes, your honor. I would like to move for a directed verdict for the defendant. There's no evidence that any kind of sexual activity happened on the estate of Carl Williams at any time, and there's ample evidence all the girls at these parties were lying about their age. They all had fake IDs because they wanted to make money off my client. He's a victim in all this. He can't come back to the United States because of all the lies and deception. So I'd like a directed verdict now. If this circus of a trial is allowed to go forward, my client will be prejudiced."

I just looked at Jonathan and wondered if he knew *anything* about trying a case. I looked at the judge, who was staring at Jonathan with a look on his face that said "this guy can't be this stupid."

But maybe he was.

"Counselor, you do know that I cannot enter a directed verdict until I've at least had the chance to hear the plaintiff's evidence, right?" Judge Foster asked disbelievingly.

"I do know that usually that's the way it goes, but this is exigent circumstances. If this trial goes on, my client will be defamed on the stand. I'd like to prevent that from happening, that is all."

Judge Foster sat back in his chair and put his hand on his chin. "Mr. Augusto, I'm tempted right now to hold you in contempt of court. You are disrespecting this court by showing up here three sheets to the wind, and I can smell the vodka coming from that water bottle of yours. I refuse to believe you don't know the basic rules of evidence, and, if you are truly serious about your motion for a directed verdict, then I'm afraid I'm going to have to at least order you take 20 hours of continuing legal education courses that focus on legal procedure."

Was this guy for real? Was he really that terrible of an attorney? Or was he trying to lay a trap? Reel me in, make me think that this case was going to be cake, and then run away with the case because I had a false sense of confidence.

Whatever. I would approach this case the same way, no matter if the guy was a total idiot or not. But, at the moment, it looked like this guy truly was a moron.

"Okay, then," Judge Foster said. "For now, I'll not hold you in contempt of court. However, if you show up drunk again tomorrow, I will reconsider. And I hope, for the sake of your client, that you get your act together, Mr. Augusto. I will now call in the jury pool."

Chapter Thirty-Four

FOR THE NEXT SIX HOURS, I questioned the jury pool about various aspects of the case. I only needed 9 people to get a verdict, not all 12, so I knew that I could afford there to be three people who weren't on my side and would never be. I also knew I didn't have to prove my case beyond a reasonable doubt. I only needed to prove it was more likely than not my case was true. The standard was called "preponderance of the evidence," and the burden of proof was considerably less than in a criminal case.

I obviously wanted to get a certain kind of juror. I wanted as many moms on the jury as possible. I especially wanted moms who had daughters at home. If those daughters were minor children, all the better. While I couldn't possibly get an entire jury made up of mothers of young daughters, if I could just get a few women who could imagine their own child up on the stand, testifying about doing disgusting things with older men who were exploiting them, I'd be golden.

I did manage to get four such women on the jury, after

everything was said and done. One was black, one was Hispanic, and two were white. The other jurors were made up of men, women without children, and two senior citizens.

Overall, though, I got the jury I wanted.

Now it was time to shine.

Chapter Thirty-Five

THE NEXT DAY, it was time to get the case underway. My opening statement was first. I went through the facts, methodically, step by step. I told the jury about what they would hear, and I warned them that it would be disturbing. To say the very least. I told them about Carl, about how he charged his clients $50,000 a month, therefore this ring was extremely elite, and that he must not be able to get away with doing what he was doing to these girls. The criminal justice system can't hold him to account, at least not until the guy was extradited from Sweden, and I made sure the jury knew the prosecutors were not trying very hard to get Carl over here to face charges.

In other words, if they didn't bring Carl to justice, he would get away with it completely. They couldn't let that happen.

And then came Jonathan's opening statement. Jonathan didn't seem drunk at that moment, so that was clearly a step up from the previous day. But that was all I could say about his performance.

"There's not a single shred of evidence that any sexual activity happened on Mr. Williams' estate, not a scintilla," he thundered, his face getting redder and redder, while a vein popped out of his forehead. He was breathing heavily and he groaned as he moved around the courtroom. "Were there parties? Sure, there were parties. Lots of parties. Fun parties, too. Men would come from all over the country, from other countries, even, to attend these parties. But sex? No, nobody was having sex at these parties. Mr. Williams was very clear that if anybody had sex on his premises, that person would be asked to leave and never come back."

"And these girls who attended these parties, they were underaged, sure. But they all presented with fake IDs. How can you tell a girl is underaged these days? Kids grow up fast these days, they really do, and I can't tell you how many 13 year olds are running around who could pass for 25. This is a different age these days, a different time from when you and I were growing up. Hell, men are passing for women, women passing for men, we got men in the ladies bathroom and vice-versa these days. You can't tell who's a male and who's a female, and you can't tell who's an adult female and who's a child. You know that's true. So when my client hired girls to entertain these men at these parties, and again, all these girls did were entertain the men, these girls gave my client IDs saying they were 21. My client took them at their word. And remember, they didn't have sex with these men, ever. They just flirted with them, made them feel good. They fluffed up the male ego, we men have fragile egos, you know, and these young girls made these men feel young."

"So, that's all it was. These men showed up at the parties because they wanted to feel young, and swimming in a beautiful heated saltwater pool with young girls made them feel that way. Flirting with young girls and having them flirt back, that was good for their egos. That was all it was. Just a lot of fragile male egos being propped up by beautiful young women, young women who lied about how old they were. And these women, they're going to tell you they had sex with these men, but that's a lie, plain and simple. They're just trying to get money out of my client and that's why they're going to lie. Oh, you're going to hear from people who worked these parties, cooks and waitresses and people like that, and they're going to tell you they saw men kissing young women in the pool. Nothing illegal about that. Men can kiss young women consensually. And these people will talk about all the flirting going on in these parties. Again, not illegal."

"Here is what nobody will testify to on the stand. Nobody will testify that they witnessed any of these men groping or molesting these young ladies. Nobody will testify that they witnessed any kind of sexual act between these men and the ladies. Not oral and not intercourse. Nobody can testify otherwise. Well, nobody who's disinterested, anyhow. The girls, they're going to lie and say they had sex with these men, but, again, they're only after money."

"And that's the bottom line here, ladies and gentlemen. The only witnesses who will testify that there was sexual contact between men and underaged ladies are the ladies themselves. There is absolutely no unmotivated evidence that says otherwise."

"I would like all of you to set aside your prejudices and forget about what you've heard about this case. Everything you've heard in the media has been lies, damned lies. Thank you very much."

He sat down and I drew a breath. I looked over at the jury and saw their expressions were changed. I also noticed that, while Jonathan was talking about the fragile male ego and how nobody could testify there was sex involved, jury members were looking at each other and nodding.

They weren't going to fall for that BS, were they?

They just might. Jonathan was right about one thing. I deposed everybody involved in these parties, all the waitresses, all the hostesses, and Jacqueline Price, the "house mother," and none of them actually saw evidence of groping or molesting, let alone hard evidence about sexual contact.

I saw in their faces that they might fall for that BS.

And if they did, I would be in trouble.

ably can't be prosecuted, but if you could bring him down in civil court, I'm all for it. How much money you talking?"

"With punitives, I'm asking for $500 million. I'm representing 100 victims. I'm going to try to get them certified as a class. I contacted all the girls exploited by Carl, going back 20 years. Not all of them are eligible to sue, though, because of statute of limitation issues, but I'm getting as many on board as I can. I figure that $5 million apiece won't exactly make them whole, but maybe it will give them a sense of justice."

"Okay then, consider it done. And thank you for saving my daughter. I didn't know what she was up to. She never told me anything about that. I guess she was afraid to. But when she got out of Carl's house, she came to see me. I'll do anything for her. But her mother, that's another story. She could burn in hell for all I care."

———

FIVE DAYS LATER, I got a call from Jonathan. "Well played, counselor. Well played. Respect for the alpha queen. I guess I'll be seeing you in court, and, don't worry, you won't see any more dirty tricks from me. For the first time in my life, I guess I'm going to have to play it straight."

"I guess so," I said. "Now, shall we exchange discovery deadlines, or do we need to go to court to do so? I also need you to make your client available for a deposition prior to trial. I know you can make that happen. I don't even care that he's lazing around in Sweden, hiding out from all the people here who hate him, which encompasses just about everyone. You will make him available on a date certain. I'll issue the subpoena. You will keep to the calendar the judge will set for us in our case management conference. You got that?"

"Yes, ma'am," Jonathan said.

"Thought so."

JUST AS I TOLD JONATHAN, I subpoenaed Carl for a deposition. Jonathan was behaving himself and acting as a true opposing counsel and not a thug.

Funny how the threat of death changes a person's attitude.

We went through our first case management conference with the judge assigned to this case. The judge's name was Judge Richard Foster, a 20-year veteran. I was excited to have drawn him. Ordinarily, I didn't necessarily want him as a judge because he was no-nonsense and known to be a prosecutor's judge. But, in this case, I wanted him, because he was also considered to be a plaintiff's judge. That seemed to be a contradiction, until I found out he started his legal career working for a personal injury firm and his parents were killed in a robbery gone wrong. When I learned his background, his predelictions made much more sense.

Our case management conference took place in the judge's chambers. Judge Foster took one look at Jonathan and I could tell, just by looking at Judge Foster's face when he saw him, that his reputation preceded him.

"Mr. Augusto," Judge Foster said, a look of disgust on his face. "I'm surprised to see you on a case here. I thought you just threatened everybody not to file a case and that's how you got things done."

I had to suppress a smile. *This was getting off to a good start.*

I liked the fact that this judge held Jonathan in such disdain. It probably would help me in the end.

Jonathan just laughed it off. "I don't always use the intimidation method. I'll be on this case legitimately, you can be guaranteed about that."

"I'll take you at your word. Anyhow, Ms. Collins, Mr. Augusto, let's set this case for trial, although I would like the parties to go to mediation sometime between now and then. Let's get a calendar set for discovery to be completed as well. I assume that, at this moment, there's not a possibility of a settlement?"

"No, your honor," I said. "As you can see from my pleadings, I'm asking for substantial punitive damages in this case. $500 million. Therefore, I don't see any possibility this case will settle before trial."

Judge Foster looked right at Jonathan. "Mr. Augusto, what say you? Ms. Collins makes a good point. She's asking for punitive damages, which will probably be the bulk of what a jury will award her and her clients, and, by the way, are you going to try to certify your clients as a class? I have to assume you will be with so many clients."

"Yes. I don't think I want to try 100 cases," I said with a laugh.

"Well, then, let's set a hearing for the class certification."

The judge set deadlines for exchanging discovery, and set a hearing for the class certification issue. He set us up for a possible mediation and then set the case for trial.

After the case management conference, Jonathan and I walked out of the courthouse and Jonathan looked at me. I could tell he was so tempted to go back to his usual bullying playbook. He was itching to plant some more drugs on my person, or hack into my computer and plant a virus in there. He wanted to throw a dead hooker in my bed, take pictures, and call the cops. I had the feeling he didn't really know how to be an actual, above-board attorney.

I knew there was the good possibility this case would be easier to win than I originally thought it would be.

"Well, Jonathan," I said. "We have our deadlines and our marching orders. And you are in receipt of a subpoena for Carl's deposition. We can agree to a video deposition if you like. I know it would be a burden for him to have to fly back here from Sweden just for a deposition, so I'll agree to that."

"I'll be quashing that subpoena," he said.

"You won't be. I just told you I'll agree to a video deposition. If I demanded he flew back from Sweden, you could quash it. But I'm being more than reasonable. Now it's up to you to set it up."

At that, I walked away. He could try to play his games all he wanted. I knew the law and procedure.

I thought he probably couldn't say the same.

Chapter Thirty-Six

THE FIRST PERSON I decided to call was Steven Barnes. He was the accountant for Carl, and he was the guy who could testify that the amount collected for dues from these men was $50,000 a month. I briefly let Jonathan's unexpectedly strong opening statement rile me, but then I knew it was up to me to show it was against common sense that these men would show up to these parties and not have sex with these women.

Who would pay $50,000 a month to attend a party where the only thing that was getting stroked was your ego? I mean, really. Come on, now. Who would pay that kind of money to merely flirt and kiss young girls?

And this accountant would also testify the girls were paid good money to "entertain" these men. They were paid $1000 a party, each girl. It beggared belief the girls were paid that kind of money if all they were doing was flirting and kissing these men. And I also knew the staff would testify that the men would disappear with the girls for long periods of time. That was circumstantial evidence right there that sex acts were happening.

Steven Barnes was tall, with a receding hairline, a long nose and was bespectacled in cool-looking black-rimmed Roberto Cavalli glasses. He was around 40 years old and was definitely nerd-hot.

He took the stand, took the oath, stated his name, and I got to work.

"Now, Mr. Barnes, you're the accountant for Carl Williams, is that correct?"

"Yes, that's correct. Mr. Williams was a client of my firm, and various accountants worked on various aspects of his businesses. He has a lot of interests in a lot of different businesses, and my role was as the accountant for his, I guess I should say it was his party business."

"And by party business, you mean?"

"Mr. Williams held parties almost every night of the week, and men paid a monthly fee to be a part of these parties. And these parties, since they were money-making ventures, were considered by my firm to be a separate business. And I was the accountant for this business venture."

I snorted a little bit when he talked about the pedophilia ring as a "business venture," and as his "party business." Is that what they were calling child rape these days?

"And how much did the clients of this business pay as a monthly fee?"

"They paid $50,000 a month," he said.

"Every client paid the same?"

"Yes. That was the membership fee, if you will, for the men who wanted to attend these parties."

"And is that amount usual, in your experience? Have you ever had the experience of accounting for a business where men would pay $50,000 per month simply for the privilege of attending parties?"

"Well, no, I've never seen that before. I've accounted for businesses that charged membership fees for different things, but not that large of a monthly amount, no."

"Would you say it was unusual that men would pay $50,000 per month just for the privilege of attending parties, then?"

"Yes, very unusual."

"Like, for instance, you've accounted for country clubs, right?"

"Right. I have."

"And how much are average dues at a country club?"

"Less than $1,000 a month, plus an initiation fee," he said. "I've also accounted for elite golf clubs, some of the most elite in the world, and the highest initiation fee for the most exclusive golf club is $500,000. But even that golf club doesn't charge a monthly fee as high as Mr. William's fee."

"And the men who were a part of Mr. Williams' party business had to sign a one-year contract, isn't that right?"

"Right. They were obligated to sign a one-year contract, yes."

"So, basically, these men were paying $600,000 a year dues, isn't that right?"

"Yes, that's correct."

"And the girls who attended these clubs, they got paid, right?"

"Right."

"And how much were they paid?"

"Typically each girl was paid $1,000 a party."

"And how many clients did Mr. Williams have at a given time?"

"He capped his clients at 100."

"So, he had 100 clients, all of whom paid him $50,000 a month, then?"

"Right."

"That's $5,000,000 a month for him, isn't it?"

"Right."

"$60 million a year?"

"Correct."

"And do you know how many years Mr. Williams has been doing his party business?"

"10 years."

"So, $60 million a year times 10. That would be $600 million he's made over the past ten years off his girls. Isn't that right?"

"Correct. I mean, that's gross, of course. Net was much less, as he had a lot of expenses, such as paying the girls $1,000 a night, and paying his staff. But yes, it was definitely a profit-making venture."

"I have nothing further."

I sat down and Jonathan stood up. "Now, Mr. Barnes, you stated that average country club dues are less than $1,000 a month, but that some golf clubs charge an initiation fee of $500,000. Isn't that right?"

"Right."

"And there is no initiation fee for Mr. Williams' club, isn't that right?"

"Right."

"So, even though the dues for Mr. Williams' club were $50,000 a month, or $600,000 a year, that isn't out of line with elite clubs around the world, is it? I mean, after all, there are no initiation fees, so really the men are paying the same yearly as men pay for elite clubs, maybe even less, isn't that right?"

"Right."

"Nothing further."

Huh. He didn't even try to address why the girls were making so much money at this "club."

The next few witnesses I called were the staff. I called hostesses, waitresses, cooks and anybody and everybody who saw the interactions between the girls and the men. They all testified they saw these men flirting with these women, and kissing them, but no petting. They all testified the girls disappeared with the men for hours at a time, but nobody could testify there was sex happening at Carl's house of horrors.

But I knew the jury could put two and two together.

Couldn't they?

Jacqueline Price, the house mother, was another story. She knew the truth. She spoke to the girls. They told her what was going on. However, when I did her deposition, she lied. She said under oath that none of the girls told her anything about any kind of sex happening on the Williams' grounds. She was totally unaware anything like that was happening.

I decided not to call her for that reason. She was a bad witness for me in her deposition, and she would be a bad witness for me in court.

After several days of witnesses, including my expert, who testified to the trauma that young girls face when they're subjected to sexual abuse, it was time to call the girls.

The case would truly begin.

Chapter Thirty-Seven

I KNEW that the first thing I needed to do was to make each girl as sympathetic as possible to the jury. I wanted all the members of the jury to see every girl on a stand as being their girl. To see every girl as being their daughter. That was key to making sure we won this case.

I was no longer positive we would win this case. I didn't want to believe it was possible that the jury would just find for the defendant. But I now knew it *was* possible. It was very possible, because people still had a hard time imagining that upstanding citizens, wealthy men, powerful men, could do something like that with very young girls.

So it was important to me that these girls were credible. I worked with them, for days and days. And I made sure they all dressed respectably. It was human nature to discount young girls if they looked a certain way. If the girls didn't look respectable, I was afraid the jury would think the girls asked for it. That wasn't right, in any way, shape or form. These girls, by and large, were good girls. They were troubled. They came from troubled homes, a lot of them. But they were still very young, and, at their cores, they were still innocent in a way. Carl tried to steal their innocence. He could never take away their essence.

The first girl I called was Angela Todd. Angela's curly red hair was in a ponytail, and she was dressed in a cream colored dress and flat shoes. She wore minimal makeup, as all the girls were instructed to do. She was wide-eyed and looked terrified. I felt bad. I'd prepared the girls for this moment, but nothing could ever prepare them for the reality of having to take the stand and tell their story before a jury of their peers.

After she was sworn in, I walked up to her and spoke to her in a low voice. "Remember, you don't have to go through with this if you can't. I'll understand. I know you're scared. Nothing could ever prepare you for this moment. I can almost hear your heart beating."

She shook her head, her eyes looking fearfully at the jury, and then back at me. "I'm fine. I just want to get this over with."

With a heavy heart, I walked away from the stand, and took a look at my notes. I let the jury just watch Angela on the stand for a minute or so. I wanted them to just soak in who she was, the aura she was emanating.

"Can you please state your name for the record?" I began after she was sworn in.

She nodded, and then looked over at the jury again. "Angela Michelle Todd."

"And Angela, do you understand why you are testifying in court today?"

"Yes. I understand that I'm testifying because there is a lawsuit against Carl Williams for what he did to me and a lot of other girls."

"Angela, do you know a man by the name of Carl Williams?"

She nodded her head. "Yes. I just said I'm testifying against Carl today. So yes, I do know him."

"When did you meet Mr. Williams?"

She got close to the microphone. "About a year ago."

"Prior to meeting him, were you living at home?"

"No. I wasn't." She shifted uncomfortably in her seat. "I was living with a foster family. However, I was one of five foster kids living with this family, and I was about to be removed from the home because they weren't caring for me."

"What do you mean, they weren't caring for you?"

"They didn't feed us a lot of nights. They were never home, and there was another boy in the house, about my age. And he was always harassing me. He was always trying to get me to do things to him, sexually. And one day, he actually did something to me. Against my will. And I told my foster parents what he did, and they made it out to be my fault. They told me I was teasing him and he was a young boy with hormones and needs. And this was my fifth foster family in six years. So I just decided I didn't need to be there anymore."

"So what did you do?"

"Well, one night, I just left the house. I sneaked out of the window of the bedroom and went to a bus station. I was going to go out of town, but I didn't really know where. I had a little bit of money saved up, and I had enough money for a bus ticket, and I was just gonna go someplace. I admit, I didn't know what I was gonna do when I split town. I was going to think of that later."

"And what happened when you went to the bus station?"

"I didn't actually end up getting on the bus. I started talking to a lady, her name is Jacqueline Price. I don't know, she kinda knew I was lost and alone and she started talking to me. I told her my entire story, because she asked where I was going and what I was doing. I told her about the foster family, and about all the foster families before that. I told her about all the group homes I used to live in when I was in between foster homes. See, my mom, my birth mom, she lost custody of me when I was a baby because she was into drugs. My dad, he was imprisoned, and he died in prison. So I told her that whole story. And she told me she had a place for me to stay. A very nice place for me to stay. And I figured I had nothing to lose. So I just went along with her."

"And where did you end up going that night?" I asked her.

"She took me to this beautiful home, mansion, estate, in Del Mar. I'd never seen a place like that before in my entire life. Well, except for on TV. Or in magazines, you know, when they would run pictures of the rich and famous. That was the kind of home it was. And she led me to this house that was kind of off to the side, kind of by the pool area, it was a big house too. Six bedrooms. And there were a bunch of girls in this house, just kind of sitting around the living room, eating pizza and watching movies. And she told me I could live there. I had no place else to go, so that place seemed like heaven."

"Did she tell you what you had to do to live in that place?"

"No. She just told me it was a safe place for girls like me. And that's all she told me. I thought it was a dream come true. I thought it was too good to be true, but at the same time, I wanted it to be true."

"What happened next?"

"I just hung out with the girls in the living room that night. And Jacqueline, she showed me where I would be sleeping. It was a twin bed, a bunk bed, and I was sharing it with another girl by the name of Naomi King. It was a much nicer room than I have ever experienced in my life. And, for the first time in a while, I was actually getting fed. They would bring in food, but also they had the chefs that would cook for us girls. And just for the next week or so, I just hung around that house, that guest house, and I thought it was the best thing ever for me."

"Did you start going to parties?"

She lowered her head. I could see she was shaking, and I felt for her. "Yes. After about a couple weeks of me hanging around the house, I kept waiting for them to ask me to leave, but they didn't. And I was invited to my first party one Monday night."

"Who attended this party?"

"Well, there were about 20 girls at the party. They were all young, like me. About my age. And there were a bunch of like, men, who were like, they were at least like 40. I would say that probably the youngest guy there was 40. Sometimes there were younger guys there, about 30 or so. But that night, it seemed like every man was over the age of 40."

"Did Jaqueline tell you what your role would be at that party?"

"Yes. She told me I was supposed to just talk to these men, and flirt with them. I didn't really know what she was talking about, but she told me to watch the other girls, and kind of watch what they were doing. So I did. The guys would come and talk to me, and I flirted with them, just like she said. She told me to touch their arm, touch their shoulder, play with their hair. Giggle a lot. It all seemed kinda silly. But I did what I was told I had to do."

"So, that first night, did you end up kissing any of the men?"

"No. Jacqueline, she went around telling every man that this is my first night. They all seemed to understand what that meant. I think what that meant to them was that I was new, so I was just learning what was going on. But I wasn't actually learning at all, I was just thinking I was supposed to be entertaining these men somehow. That's what I was told I had to do."

"During this party, did you notice other girls disappearing with other men?"

"Yeah. I noticed that all through the night, one girl after another would disappear with one man after another. And they would be gone for like an hour, sometimes more. Sometimes less. And they would come back to the party, and sometimes that same guy would disappear with another girl. I saw that happening, and I asked the girls where they went. And they would just laugh and giggle and say they were walking around the grounds. And Carl, he does have a lot of land, and there's a cliff, where you can sit there and look at the ocean below. There's just a lot to see. So I just figured those girls were just walking around the grounds, maybe going to look at the ocean. And there's some steps to go down to the ocean and some of the girls said they would go down to the beach with a man and just kind of walk around. And I didn't think anything was going on that was wrong."

"And how long did you attend these parties?"

"Well, for the first month, I just attended the parties and didn't do anything with these men at all. I just flirted with them, like Jacqueline told me to do. And I was still thinking it was a really nice set up for me. I mean, I was staying at a really nice place, going to parties every night, making a lot of friends. Eating a lot of good food. So it was just kind of like paradise."

"After that first month, what happened?"

"Jacqueline told me I would have to leave."

"She said you would have to leave?"

"Yes. That's what she told me."

"Did she tell you why you had to leave?"

"Yes. She said I had to leave because they would be bringing in a new girl and they needed the bed."

"What did you do?"

"I panicked. I had no place to go. And no money. And I was having such a nice time at that house. Making a lot of close friends. I panicked."

"Did you leave?"

"No," she said with a shake of her head. Then she bowed her head again. "I didn't."

"And why didn't you leave?"

"I didn't leave because I started to cry. And then Jacqueline said there was a way I could stay with the other girls. And she said I could make some money as well."

"And did she tell you what you had to do to stay there?"

"Yes. She said that if I wanted to stay there, I needed to do more at these parties. She told me that at these parties that I was to go with any man who asked me, into a private place, in the main house, and that I was to do anything they asked me once I went with them."

"Did you understand at that time that she wanted you to prostitute yourself with these men?"

"At first I didn't understand. I didn't even think that's what she was asking me to do. So, I asked her questions, and she answered that I had to do whatever the men asked me to do. And then she said that if I did that, I would get paid $1000 for every party I attended where I allowed myself to go with these men to a private room."

"And what did you say?"

"I said I didn't want to do that. She said that was fine, that I would have to leave, because they would get a new girl in there who would be willing to do those things." She bowed her head, tears in her eyes. "I couldn't leave there. I just didn't know what I would do if I had to leave that place. I didn't have any place to go. I couldn't go back into the system. I'd been through so many foster homes and none of them were any good. In some of those homes, I was beaten. In some of those homes, the parents, the foster parents, they were doing a lot of drugs. Some of the homes were okay, but they just had too much going on and didn't have time for me. I never felt I had a family until I got to Carl's house. I felt like I was part of a family there because I bonded with the other girls. They became like my sisters. I didn't want to leave them. I just didn't know what to do."

"So, what happened next?"

"Jacqueline, she gave me some time to think about what I wanted to do. I asked Naomi about what she thought. None of the girls were telling me what they were doing at these parties. They were all lying to me. Telling me nothing was going on. But, at this point, I guess they were told they could tell me the truth and Naomi told me what she was doing. She told me that it wasn't so bad once I got used to it. I just didn't imagine I would ever do something like that, but I felt like I had no choice." She bowed her head and I could see tears in her eyes. Her hands were shaking and she kept smoothing her hair, over and over again.

"So what did you decide?"

"I decided to give it a try. So, that night, at that party, I guess the guys who attended the party were told I wasn't off-limits. And about half an hour after I got to the party, an older guy came up to me. He flirted with me, and I flirted back, like I was taught to. And then he whispered in my ear that he wanted me to go with him to a private place. I had never been inside the main house, at least not before this. But it's a huge house, 20 bedrooms. I found out later that all those bedrooms were being used for these men who would be taking these young girls and doing things to them sexually in these bedrooms. And that's what happened with this guy. I was scared but I knew I had to do it."

I didn't want to ask her the dirty details, but at the same time, I had to get her testifying on the record that there was sexual contact between her and this man. "When you went into this private room with this man, was there sexual contact?"

She took a deep breath and looked furtively at the jury. I looked behind me and saw every member of the jury was transfixed on her face. "Yes. There was. He asked me to give him a blow job, and I did. And then he asked me to take off my clothes, and he took off his clothes, and he had sex with me."

"Intercourse?"

She nodded her head. "Yes."

"And how old were you when this happened?"

"16."

She took a deep breath. I could tell she was choking back a sob.

"How did you feel after doing that?"

"I felt dirty. Ashamed. I couldn't believe this was my life. That this was what things had come to. I mean, I wasn't a virgin or anything like that. But, I never thought I'd be doing something like that with some random guy I just met, for money. It was just wrong."

"And did you keep doing that – going to parties, meeting men, and having sexual encounters with them?"

She nodded her head. "Yes. I did. And it wasn't as bad once I started getting into it. I mean, the first time was the worst time. And I was told at some point I would have to keep a quota. I had to go with three different men every night, to a private place, and do what they wanted me to do. Whatever they wanted me to do."

"So, if a guy said he wanted a three-way with you, you had to do it?"

"Yes. That was something that happened quite a lot. A guy would choose me and another girl at the party, and all three of us would, you know. All three of us would have sex together."

"And if a guy said that he wanted to urinate on you, you had to do that as well?"

She nodded. "Yes. I was told I couldn't refuse any request. If I did refuse a request, they would get rid of me. So yes, if the guy requested to pee on me, I had to let him do it. In fact, it did. At least five times."

"So, you're telling the court that men have urinated on you?"

She nodded her head. "Yes. I had to go along with anything a man wanted."

"How did you feel after Carl told you and all the girls that you could leave at any time?"

"At first I was afraid. I didn't know what I was going to do. None of us knew what to do. It was a terrible way of living, but it was the only way we knew. But then you saved us. You got us a group home, in therapy, and people to take care of us. And we have each other, which is the most important thing."

"Did you give Carl a fake ID at any time?"

"No, ma'am," she said. "I don't have a fake ID."

"How do you feel now about men?"

"I don't know. I don't have any feelings at all for men. I don't have any feelings for boys, either. I mean, I just turned 17, and I can't ever imagine going on a date with anybody. Just the thought of being alone with any man or boy makes me want to vomit."

"I have nothing further for this witness."

Angela looked terrified, because she knew Jonathan was going to cross-examine her. I told her to be careful because he was going to try to trip her up.

Jonathan took a deep breath and he looked frustrated. "Your Honor, I'd like to have a short recess. If you may."

Judge Foster nodded and then banged the gavel. "Ladies and gentlemen of the jury, we're going to take a short break. About 10 minutes. Ms. Todd, I would like for you to remain seated. Mr. Augusto, Ms. Collins, why don't you come on back to my chambers."

Jonathan and I followed Judge Foster into the chambers.

"Okay, counselor, what's on your mind?" Judge Foster asked Jonathan.

"I can't possibly cross-examine that girl. If I do, the jury will think I'm some monster."

"Well, you're going to have to cross-examine her if you want any chance at all of winning for your client," Judge Foster said. "I really don't understand why you decided to call a recess just to tell me that you're going to have a hard time cross-examining a witness."

"I guess what I'm saying is that I need to confer with my client about this case. I need to talk to him tonight and it's 4 o'clock in the afternoon right now. I think we can probably quit for the day. Maybe, tomorrow, I can cross-examine her? We can recall her tomorrow, can't we?"

"If that's what you want to do," Judge Murphy said. "I'll tell the jury we're recessing for the evening and we'll be back tomorrow at 9 AM sharp."

"Thank you," Jonathan said to Judge Murphy.

All of us left the chambers and the judge took the bench. When the jury came back, Judge Murphy informed the jury they were free to go. "Be back tomorrow morning right at 9," he admonished. "And, Ms. Todd, you are excused for now. However, tomorrow, you will take the stand again when we get started. You will remain under oath. Thank you very much and I'm sorry for the inconvenience."

Angela looked at me with a bewildered expression on her beautiful face. "I don't understand?" she said.

"You're excused for now," I said. "But the first thing tomorrow, I'm going to call you again to testify."

"Okay," she said. Her brow furrowed and she was extremely hesitant about getting out of her seat. She looked around the courtroom and then tentatively stood up. "What just happened?" she asked me as she walked past the plaintiff's table.

"I'll tell you later," I said.

Angela left the courtroom and I packed up my evidence. We were done for the day.

But why?

Chapter Thirty-Eight

JONATHAN

JONATHAN AUGUSTO LEFT the courtroom feeling shaken. He wasn't used to actually trying cases. That much was evident. His MO was always, always, to intimidate the other side into dropping the case. By any means possible. That was how he operated. That was what he was paid the big bucks for. And that was how he'd assumed he would go about this case, too. When Carl hired him, he hired him with the full knowledge that he would do what it took to make sure the case was dismissed with prejudice.

When he explained to Carl that he would have to try this case legitimately, he was surprised Carl kept him on. But he did. "You're a ruthless person outside the courtroom. I expect you to be just as ruthless inside it." That's what he said. He expected him to bellow and holler and object to every single utterance that came out of Avery Collins' mouth. He expected him to lie and get witnesses to lie and encourage everybody to commit perjury on Carl's behalf.

And it worked, in a way. Jacqueline Price lied under oath in her deposition, because Carl threatened her that if she didn't lie, she would go to prison for her role in Carl's ring. And that was the truth. Jacqueline had to play dumb. She had to pretend she had no clue on what was happening. Because she played along, Jonathan was able to get the prosecutors to agree not going to prosecute her.

And, of course, he lied between his teeth in his opening statement. He damn well knew that Carl's parties were sex trafficking parties. Hell, he'd even been to a party a time or two and partook in the lovely ladies himself. He knew the girls were underaged. Everybody knew the girls were underaged. That was the whole point of being a part of Carl's ring. It was the excitement of having sex with very young girls. Carl would never have been able to charge as much money as he did if the girls were all 21 and over. What fun is that? You can get that anywhere. But Carl supplied girls who couldn't be gotten anywhere, not legally, and he provided the protection of the Russian mob behind it. Nobody would prosecute him or any of the guys who came to these parties, either, because Carl just had too many friends in high places.

But when that young girl took the stand and Jonathan got a look at her…it wasn't good. She looked so young, so small, even though she was a tall one, almost 5'9". But she looked frail. And devastated. The fact that her life was probably ruined showed on her face and in her body language.

And her testimony… he didn't know how he was supposed to counteract that. He saw the jury. He saw how they looked at Angela. Every single one of them had pity in their eyes. Even some of the hardened ones, the ones he thought would be good for him, they just weren't.

Angela was everybody's daughter, sister, and friend in their eyes. And Jonathan would have to try to trip her up and all the other girls Avery Collins had lined up to testify, four of them in all. But if the other girls were as affecting as Angela, Jonathan had a feeling that Carl would be in for a rude awakening. Avery was only asking for $500 million, most of which was punitive damages, although she was also asking for compensatory damages for pain, suffering and emotional distress. This money would be spread out between 100 victims.

He would have to lay it on the line with Carl. He doubted the jury would stop at $500 million. Not when Carl was worth 30 times that. Avery had the information about Carl's net worth, because Carl provided it to her when Avery subpoenaed him. She could show the jury that Carl could afford to pay any judgment, and that he had made well over $500 million off his girls over the years. He typically had 100 clients on his list, with more on a waiting list, and each client paid $50,000 per month. That meant he was bringing in $5 million a month, $60 million a year, and had been at this for the past 20 years. That jury would do the math and might ding him for a billion or more.

He could see it happening.

———

"HEY CARL," he said when he video-called him, knowing it was well past 3 in the morning there. It couldn't be helped.

Carl's face was sleepy and irritated. "Yeah? Why are you calling me so late?"

"It's not late here. It's only past 6. Listen, I don't know about going forward with this case. That Angela Todd, you didn't see her on the stand. Everybody in the jury box looked like they were going to cry. I don't have a good feeling about this, not at all. Listen, Avery Collins, she's only asking for $500 million. You make that much money in your sleep. Why don't we just settle with her, get this case off the front page so you can live your life again, and call it a day?"

"No. We talked about this. I don't settle cases. Not cases like this. There's no proof that anything untoward happened at my house. None at all. Except for the testimony of a bunch of bitches who have dollar signs in their eyes. You got this. All you got to do is make those whores look like the lying bitches they are. You rip them up, limb from limb. You eat them up and spit out their skinny bones. Stay the course and we'll win this thing."

Jonathan was sorry that he had video-called Carl, because he knew his facial expression was one of disbelief. This guy was delusional.

"You're not listening to me. You could be on the hook for a billion dollars when all of this is said and done. I think you should settle."

"No settlement. None. Now, I have to get to bed. I have a lot of work to do in the morning."

At that, Carl cut off the call.

Jonathan had a bad feeling about all of this.

But he had his marching orders. He had to try to nail those girls to the wall.

And he was going to do it.

He just hoped it didn't backfire on him.

Chapter Thirty-Nine

THE NEXT DAY, Angela got back on the stand, and Jonathan was loaded for bear. "Ms. Todd, you testified that you had to have sex with various men while in the employ of my client, Carl Williams, isn't that right?"

"Right."

"But nobody ever saw you actually having sex with these men, did they?"

"No, I mean, the men saw me, obviously. And when I did three ways, those other girls who were involved, they saw me."

"But those other girls you were doing three-ways with, they're also a part of this lawsuit, aren't they?"

"Yes, of course they are."

"So, they're motivated to lie as well, aren't they? They want money too, don't they?"

"I'm not lying. Nobody is going to lie about what happened at that house."

"But isn't it true that your attorney actually hasn't called any of the men, the clients, to testify?"

"I don't know, you'll have to ask her."

"I can assure you that none of the men who took part in these parties are on her witness list. They wouldn't be motivated to lie, so they would tell the truth, wouldn't you agree?"

Angela shook her head. "They would be really motivated to lie, because if they told the truth, they'd be arrested."

I had to smile. She was a smart cookie, that one.

"Now you admitted on the stand that you weren't a virgin when you arrived at Carl's house, isn't that right?"

I was immediately on my feet. "Objection, relevance."

"Sustained. Move along, counselor."

"You stated on direct that you sneaked out of a foster home. Did you actually ever talk to your foster family after that?"

"Yes I did."

"And what did you say to them?"

"I told them I was staying with a friend and not to worry."

"Oh, so you lied to them, did you?"

"I guess so."

"And lying comes easy to you, doesn't it?"

"No it doesn't."

"It doesn't? Yet you just said you told your foster family, as easy as you please, that you were staying with a friend, when, in truth, you were staying with Mr. Williams. That lie came easily enough to you. This lie is coming just as easy, isn't it?"

"But I'm not lying. I promise you, I'm telling the God's honest truth."

"And why didn't you go to the police when Jacqueline told you what you had to do with these men?"

"I don't know. I wanted to stay there. I didn't want to leave. I had no place to go. I-" She hung her head. "I should have called the police. I should have. But I didn't. I'm sorry."

"Right. Didn't your parents ever tell you that you're supposed to call the police when you see somebody doing something wrong?"

"No. My parents never taught me anything like that. My mom was a drug addict and my father was in prison, where he died. I've been in and out of foster families my entire life. Nobody ever taught me right from wrong."

"Aha! So, you admit you don't know right from wrong, then?"

"Well, no, I'm not admitting that, but I'm just saying that nobody close to me ever taught me about that."

"And nobody ever taught you lying is wrong, either, did they?"

"Well, no, but I know lying is wrong."

"You must not know lying is wrong, because here you are, lying on the stand."

"I'm not lying." Angela was clearly getting frustrated. "I'm not lying. There's going to be three other girls who are all going to say the same type of thing I'm saying. All of them. There are a lot more girls who can testify to the same thing, but they won't be, because most of them are pretty messed up about the whole thing. But I'm not lying. They won't be lying, either."

"Do you have money to live on, Ms. Todd?"

"No, I don't. Not right now. I'm living in that group home, and I'm being taken care of there, but once I get out of there, I don't know how I'm going to make ends meet."

"But don't you agree that a big windfall in this case will help you out immensely?"

"I don't understand."

"I mean, if you get, say, a million dollars from this case, you'll be set for life, won't you? You're not going to have to worry about a thing. But if you don't get this money, you'll be struggling your whole life, wouldn't you agree?"

"I guess. But that's not why-"

"I have nothing further."

Angela looked at the judge with a dazed look in her eyes.

"Ms. Todd, you are excused."

"Thanks," she said.

Chapter Forty

FOR THE NEXT THREE DAYS, I called my witnesses to testify. Dakota Murphy, Cameron Hayes and Naomi King all testified similarly to Angela. Their stories were not exactly identical, but only because they all had different stories on how they came to meet Carl in the first place.

Naomi talked about how she was introduced into the circle by her cousin, who already was in the circle. Dakota talked about how her mother was friends with Carl and suggested Dakota work for him - she had a similar story to Emma, Harrison's daughter, who also was sold into prostitution by her own money-hungry mother. Cameron talked about how she ran away from her abusive home and was found by a Russian by the name of Oleg Karinsky, and Oleg brought her in.

Their stories were different on how they found the place, but, once they got there, their stories were remarkably similar. They each told the court about how they hung back for a month or more, while Jacqueline groomed them for bigger and better things, even though they weren't aware this was what was happening. They each told the court about how they were asked to leave, but given a chance to stay only if they would start providing sexual favors to the men at the parties. They each told the court about how they reluctantly started doing that because they didn't know what else they could do.

And Jonathan tried, with each girl, to show they were lying. But I could almost tell his heart wasn't in it. How could it be? Jonathan knew the score. I knew he knew. By the end of the girls' testimonies, I could tell he was phoning it in, exhausted by having to use the same tactics to try to trip up four virtually identical tales of being trafficked to the rich and famous.

And each girl testified they didn't provide a fake ID to anyone.

FINALLY, after six days of grueling testimony, and Jonathan not even trying to put on his own evidence to refute it, it was time for closing arguments. Jonathan didn't have his own evidence. He couldn't call any of the men to say the girls were all lying bitches, because none of them were willing to testify. And Carl wasn't willing to testify, either, although I did have his videotaped deposition where he lied the entire time. I elected not to show the jury that, and Jonathan didn't, either, so the whole thing just died on the vine.

I went first with my closing argument.

"Okay, ladies and gentlemen," I began. "Let me remind you about what Mr. Augusto, the attorney for the defendant, told you in his opening statement. He told you there was no proof that anything illegal was happening at Carl Williams' home. That the most that happened was that the men kissed some underaged girls, and kissing's not illegal. Well, now, you heard the testimony of four of the young ladies who were a part of this sex trafficking ring. You heard them. You got a look at them. Did they look like ladies who were motivated by money?"

"And I want you to consider just a few aspects of this case. I want to highlight them, if you will. First, the accountant for Carl Williams admitted on the stand that Carl has 100 men pay him $50,000 every month for his party services," I said, putting air quotes around the words "party services." "Come on, now, $50,000 a month for the chance to kiss an underage girl? Really? Do you believe that for two seconds? It doesn't cost $50,000 a month to belong to the most elite golf club or country club in the world. Yet, these men, these wealthy and powerful men, were willing to shell that money out for some chaste kisses and some walks in the moonlight?"

I shook my head. "No. That's not right and you know it's not right. In what world would that happen? Not in this one and you know it. You know these men wouldn't pay that much money unless it was for the chance to get something they can't just get anywhere. And that means these men were paying for the chance to have sex with beautiful underaged women, as many beautiful underaged women as they wanted. You heard the girls testify to just that."

"Plus, the accountant, Mr. Steven Barnes, testified that the girls were all paid $1000 per party. That was Mr. Barnes' testimony. Now is Carl Williams going to pay his girls $1,000 a party just so they can flirt with the men and give them some kisses and a chance to play chicken with them in the pool? Is that what believe about this case?"

I had the jury right at that moment. I could see it in their faces.

"No. Ladies and gentlemen, you're smart. You're too smart to believe the nonsense that the defense counsel wants you to believe. You have common sense, same as anybody else, and your common sense is telling you that Carl Williams was sex trafficking underaged girls. Plain and simple."

"And let me remind you that punitive damages are available for this case. Punitive damages are designed to punish a defendant. To tell the defendant his behavior is not acceptable in any way, shape or form. To tell the defendant his behavior won't be tolerated in society. I urge you to punish this man, because this is the only way Mr. Williams will be brought to justice for what he has done. I ask for compensatory damages for the entire class of girls, 100 in all, of $20 million. This for their pain, suffering and emotional distress. And another $480 million in punitive damages. Remember, Carl Williams was grossing $60 million a year off these women and he's been doing it for the past 20 years. Send him a message by stripping him of almost all he's grossed with these young ladies over the years. That would be his just desserts. Thank you very much."

I sat down, and Jonathan stood up. He reiterated the same things he said in his opening statement. He once again talked about how the girls were lying, there was no proof, the girls had motive to lie, and the men at the parties just wanted to be around young girls to feel young again. There wasn't anything new that he said in his closing argument, compared to his opening statement, because he didn't present any new evidence.

And that was that. Judge Foster gave the jury instructions, telling the jury what the elements were of the intentional tort of sexual battery, how they were to calculate compensatory damages and punitive damages.

Now it was time for the waiting game.

Chapter Forty-One

THREE DAYS later and there wasn't a jury verdict yet. I hated waiting for a verdict as it was. I really hated when a jury took days to come back.

I understood why they were out, but it was still frustrating. I knew they had a lot of evidence to sift through. Days of testimony, scores of witnesses, and, to top it off, I was asking for a lot of money. Granted, $500 million wasn't that much money when you thought about what that guy did and how many victims were a part of the class.

At the same time, I was intensely interested in what was going on with the Jurgen Williams case. I was in contact with the prosecutor on that case and she was keeping me apprised on the status. Every time a motion was filed, every time discovery was exchanged, every time Beth took a deposition, I knew about it.

So I knew the case would go to trial sometime in the new year.

That case made me nervous, even more nervous than the Carl Williams case did. It had been so many years. I had given up hope I would ever get closure on that case. Now the possibility of finally finding out what happened to my best friend still seemed like an unreachable dream.

I didn't want to be disappointed. I knew Jurgen had the best hired gun money could buy defending him. Jurgen had an endless bank account and could afford the best of the best.

What if he walked?

In the meantime, I knew there was one more loose end I needed to tie up.

I had to find out about Gloria Flores, my attorney. I needed to talk to her and find out why she did what she did. Was she just overworked and incompetent, or was she dirty, too?

And if she was dirty, why? Was she bribed or blackmailed?

Or was it something else?

BY FRIDAY AFTERNOON, I got notification from the court that the jury couldn't reach a verdict and were going to try again on Monday.

I couldn't just sit around the condo on pins and needles.

I decided to get the next flight out to Kansas City. That nagging sense of unfinished business was driving me to it.

I would find out what Gloria's role was in this whole situation if it was the last thing I did.

Chapter Forty-Two

WHEN I GOT to Kansas City, I was hit in the face with the weather. It was freezing and there was about 6 inches of snow on the ground. I had just left San Diego, which was experiencing a "cold snap" where the overnight temperatures dipped to forty degrees, thus causing everybody to bundle up under electric blankets and build fires in their fireplaces, and entered into a winter wonderland.

In a way, though, it seemed more like home than San Diego ever did. It was close to Christmastime, and, out here, it actually seemed like Christmas. It wasn't just the fact that the Country Club Plaza was completely lit up in Christmas lights. Nor was it because the side of a large building on Metcalf Ave. was lit up with a large green and red wreath. It was because, well, there was snow on the ground and I never felt Christmas was Christmas without some white.

Not that I was terribly happy about the weather. For one thing, my coat, which was fine in southern California, was far too thin for subzero temperatures. For another, by the time I got into my Uber car, I was wet and couldn't feel my toes. That was what I got for impulsively coming to the midwest in the middle of December.

The first thing I did, after I dumped off my baggage in my hotel room, was rent a car. I drove straight over to Gloria's house. There wasn't time to waste as I needed to be back in San Diego on Monday, just in case the jury came back in. Besides, even though I'd waited this long to confront her, I suddenly felt I couldn't wait one second more. I had to see her face and ask her why she did what she did to me.

Gloria lived in an older section of town, the Valentine area, where the homes were grand and built around the turn of the century. Most of them were renovated, for this area was extremely gentrified. This was a mid-town neighborhood, but was definitely one that housed only yuppies.

Gloria's house was one of the larger houses on the block. The two-story house was made completely of red brick, with a giant stone porch.

As I pulled up, I was greeted by the sight of Gloria herself shoveling her driveway. I drew a breath, feeling the sense of intense anxiety grow in my chest. *Was this a good idea?*

I turned on the recorder on my phone and put it in my pocket.

Gloria glanced at my car, and then, two seconds later, looked again. Then she put her gloved hand to her mouth and immediately threw down the shovel and started to head into the house.

I got out of the car and walked rapidly towards the front door. I had to stop her before she went into the house, closed the drapes and refused to answer the door.

"Ms. Flores," I said in a loud voice.

She turned her head slowly, as if she was afraid of what she would see. "Avery, what a nice surprise," she said nervously. "What brings you to this neighborhood?"

"You. You're the only reason I'm in this city right now. I live in San Diego. But, thanks to you, I was supposed to live the rest of my life in Cameron, Missouri, as a guest of the state. It didn't quite work out that way. I found a real attorney who actually, you know, did investigative work and who, you know, actually called the medical examiner to testify that Becky was raped before she was killed. Unlike you."

I suddenly felt my anxiety change to a white-hot anger. It was something about Gloria's demeanor that brought it out. I wanted to slap her right at that moment, almost as much as I wanted to slap her after she threw my case so spectacularly.

"Avery, I'm sorry about that. But it wasn't my fault."

"Not your fault?" I suddenly forgot about how cold it was. My anger was warming me from the inside. "How was it not your fault? Did you even review the medical examiner's report? You know the ME report stated unequivocally that Becky was raped. The medical examiner did nothing wrong. The prosecutor did something wrong, because he covered up the evidence about Becky's rape. He knew I was innocent, too, but he railroaded me all the same. All you had to do was call the ME to testify and I would've been acquitted. That's all you needed to do."

"You don't understand," she said, her gloved hands flying up to her neck, straightening up the red and black scarf around it. "I had to…"

"You had to what?"

"I was going to lose my house," she said desperately. "My husband left me and I found out he had taken out five credit cards in both of our names. Fifty thousand dollars. He was gambling. Buying drugs. I couldn't file bankruptcy, because I had too much equity, and I-"

I couldn't believe what I was hearing. She literally sold me down the river. I had a feeling, but hearing her say it was something else entirely.

And then she shook her head. "Oh, what am I saying? My husband wasn't gambling. I was. I was gambling. I had a problem back then. My marriage was falling apart and I spent every weekend at the Argosy. Before I knew it, I had five credit cards, all maxed out. I was $100,000 in debt. I own this house. I couldn't file bankruptcy but I couldn't pay those credit cards."

"So you…"

"I took money from Carl Williams. You can't do anything to me about it, either, because the statute of limitations has run on my crimes. That's the only reason I'm telling you. But, yes, Carl Williams paid off my credit cards. Zero balance. And I stayed in this house."

I closed my eyes. "You couldn't have taken out a mortgage against your home to pay off the credit cards?"

Her eyes didn't meet mine. "I guess I should have."

"Damn right you should have. Oh my God. I was going to spend the rest of my life in prison because you didn't want to sacrifice your lifestyle even a little."

Her face was red. It might've been because she was ashamed of what she did. Then again, it might've been because the wind was whipping, the snow was falling, and her cheeks were chapped.

Probably the latter.

"I'm sorry," she said feebly.

"Well, there's nothing more to say, I guess. Except you're

going to lose your license to practice law. Not that you care about that, but-"

"You can't prove a thing," she said with a haughty tone. The expression on her face said *got you again.*

"You'll find out differently."

At that, I got back into my car.

Once I got back to my hotel, I immediately filed a bar complaint against her. I put her confession onto a jump drive and enclosed it in the letter.

She would be disbarred for what she did. Of that I was sure. And that would hurt. In the 20 years since Gloria threw my case, she had risen through the ranks in the Kansas City legal field, making her name in criminal defense. She was representing big-time clients who had the money to pay her large retainers. Christian found out she was clearing $500,000 a year.

I giggled a little as I realized she sold me for only $100,000, but she would be losing millions in the end, because no way would she ever be allowed to practice law in any state of the union again. State bars tend to frown on taking large bribes in exchange for throwing cases.

Looked like her decision to take that bribe would cost her one helluva lot more than $100,000.

I finally felt a sense of satisfaction and closure.

Chapter Forty-Three

I FLEW BACK to San Diego on Monday, just in time to get the text message that the jury had returned with a verdict.

My heart was in my throat as I drove to the courthouse. I didn't even stop to call the girls and tell them a verdict was in. I didn't want to see their faces if things turned out badly.

Which they might. I didn't know any other reason why the jury had taken so long to come back. I only needed 9 of the 12 to win the case, but I had no clue what they were going to do. I remembered watching a video one time when I was in law school. There were two different mock trials in front of two different mock juries. Same facts, same evidence, same lawyers in each of these cases. In one of the trials, the jury found for the plaintiff and awarded her $100 million.

In the other trial? The verdict was for the defendant.

In other words, civil trials were a crapshoot.

I felt sick as I arrived in the courtroom. Jonathan was already there, as was Judge Foster. "I'm staying at a hotel around the corner," Jonathan said. "I was right in the middle of a lunch buffet when I got the text. Damn it."

"Mr. Augusto, Ms. Collins, I will now ask the jury for their verdict,"Judge Foster said. He then addressed the jurors. "Ladies and gentlemen of the jury, have you reached a verdict in the case of King *et al.* v. Williams?" he asked.

"We have, your honor."

At that, the bailiff went to the jury foreman and got the slip of paper from him. He took the slip of paper to Judge Foster and Judge Foster looked at it. He had a poker face as he looked at whatever was on that slip of paper.

Judge Foster folded up the paper and handed it back to the bailiff, who, in turn, handed it back to the jury foreman.

Every second seemed like an hour.

"What is the verdict of the jury in the case of King *et al.* v. Williams?" Judge Foster asked.

"We the jury find in favor of the plaintiffs," the foreman began. "And we award the plaintiffs the amount of $5 billion."

Jonathan hung his head but I could see a faint smile on his face. And then he started to laugh. "I told him. I told him. I told that SOB he better settle. Woo-hee, it was even worse than I thought."

I felt stunned at the verdict. I was going to settle for $500 million. Turned out the girls were actually entitled to 10 times that.

I did a quick calculation in my head and figured out that each of the girls would get $50 million.

Good. They earned it.

And then some.

Chapter Forty-Four

THAT NIGHT, it was time to celebrate. The girls were stunned, more stunned than me. "I don't understand," Morgan, a fair-skinned brunette said to me. "We're all going to get $50 million?"

"Yes. I mean, Carl will probably try to appeal the verdict, but he has no grounds to do so. None at all. I doubt a single penny will be shaved off on appeal. At any rate, you guys won't have access to all that money right away. You're going to be appointed a special lawyer who will decide how each of you will receive the money. Most likely, it will be held in trust until your 21st birthday, but you will probably get a monthly amount until then."

Thank God the case was tried in California. Unlike many states, California had no limits on punitive damages. Some states capped them at 5x actual damages or something of the sort. Not California. Anything goes in the golden state when it came to punitives, which meant Carl had no grounds for appeal.

The girls had a lot of questions, as I knew they would. The money didn't seem real to them.

Hell, it didn't even seem real to me.

I tried to answer all their questions about the money and how they expected to receive it. They were excited and nervous as they talked all night about what to do with all that money.

"I'm going to buy an island," Rhianna said. "No, just kidding, I'm going to send a lot of money to my family. And then I'm going to buy an island."

Rhianna's birth family lived in Somalia and she came to America as an unaccompanied refugee five years ago. That money would go a long way for her family. Maybe it even meant she could be reunited with them.

"I'm going to buy a huge manse in Beverly Hills and live like a Kardashian," Naomi said excitedly.

And so on. I heard every girl express their hopes and dreams and I had to smile. They all had gone through so much.

This money could never bring back what they had lost. Their youth. Their innocence. Their sense the world wasn't a horrible place.

They would never be whole.

But it would certainly help.

Chapter Forty-Five

Three months later

LIFE WAS ACTUALLY SOMEWHAT GOOD. Gloria Flores was stripped of her license to practice law. She actually had the nerve to send me a nasty email about how I ruined her life.

I did nothing but laugh. *I* ruined *her* life?

That was rich.

And Jurgen was convicted for the murder of Becky. Beth Ahern pulled out all the stops to make sure her case against Jurgen was air-tight. Turned out the fact that you can hire the best attorney money can buy wasn't enough when all the evidence was against you.

Jurgen called me before his trial began and threatened me. "You're going to regret what you did," he said. "I can guarantee you that."

"Oh? You got some mobbed-up goons on your side again?"

At that, he hung up the phone.

No, he didn't have any mobbed-up goons on his side again. I knew that. He never had them in the first place. His daddy had the goons. His daddy was in Sweden, still not wanting a thing to do with his son.

I went out to the balcony, where Aidan was sitting in a chair, his laptop on his belly and a joint stubbed out in an ashtray on the little glass table next to the chair.

I sat down and propped my feet on the railing. "Jurgen got convicted," I said.

Aidan smiled and fist-bumped me. "I knew it would happen. I told you. All along, I told you to try to figure out who railroaded you. And you did. You did a good job, sis. A really good job."

That was true enough. I wanted to simply pull the covers over my head and try to forget my imprisonment ever happened. Aidan was always nagging me to get out there, do some investigation, bring somebody to justice.

Just do it, he said. Get it done. You'll feel better.

And he was right. Ever since I got that huge verdict against Carl, Jurgen got convicted, and Gloria lost her law license, I felt a huge weight lifted off me. I was actually sleeping at night.

Closure. Turned out it wasn't an overrated concept after all.

Next in the Southern California Legal Thrillers Series

vinci-books.com/insanity-defense

A murder, a beautiful suspect, and a skeptical lawyer.

Aidan Collins takes on his first high-profile case: defending the
alluring and unstable Marina Vasiliev, who stands accused of
murdering her wealthy spouse. With mounting evidence and
shifting loyalties, Aidan must decide whether to pursue an insanity
defense or uncover the truth behind the murder.

Turn the page for a free preview…

Insanity Defense: Chapter One

AIDAN

I WOKE up and looked at the person next to me. It was Regina. My head was splitting and I tried to desperately think about what had happened the night before. As I looked over at my nightstand, I saw a clue as to what might've happened. A joint was in the ashtray, which was pretty much par for the course for me on a Friday night. But next to the joint was an empty bottle of vodka. Grey Goose. I had pretty good taste when it came to vodka, just like my sister.

I nudged her. "Hey, you better wake up."

She turned over and looked at me, her green eyes squinting in the sunlight pouring in through the sliding glass door. She put her hand on her forehead and then put both of her hands on each side of her head, as if she was trying to steady it. She made smacking noises with her lips, as if she was trying to get something out of her mouth. Then she shook her head.

"What the hell happened? What am I doing here?" She looked down at her body, which was naked, and, I must say, beautiful. Then she looked at me. "Well, I guess that settles it. I guess you and I hit the sheets last night, although I have no idea how that happened. Maybe you can enlighten me."

There would be no enlightenment from me, unfortunately. It had been a long time since I drank to the point of blacking out, but, apparently, last night I broke that streak.

I wasn't too upset to be in bed with her. I had a crush on her from the very first time we locked eyes. But I knew she didn't feel the same about me. I knew she kind of thought of me as Avery's little brother and that was it. There was an age difference of eight years between the two of us, and I also knew she didn't date a whole lot. I knew why she never dated that much, as she had nothing but bad experiences with men over the years, so she really had no interest in getting involved with anybody.

Not that she was getting involved with me. I couldn't hope for that. The only thing I could hope for would be that maybe this could turn into an ongoing thing, a friends with benefits thing. That is if she was open to it. I had no idea if she was.

She covered herself up with a sheet and walked daintily to my attached bathroom. I looked down at her feet, as they strode across the hardwood floor, seeing how delicate they were. Her toes were painted a light pink and there were rings on just about every one of her perfect digits. On both of her ankles were tattoos. A rose with a saying on it was on her left ankle. It said *I'm not afraid, at least not to die. I'm afraid to live and not remember why.* On her right ankle was a picture of Winnie the Pooh and Christopher Robin, who was holding a balloon. I smiled, in spite of myself, seeing her tattoos. The Pooh tattoo was so unlike her, although the rose tattoo was totally her. That was her attitude - she was fearless. I would have to ask her a little later about the Pooh tattoo. Maybe it was meaningful for her, something she thought about from childhood.

I heard her rustling around in the bathroom, and I had the urge to join her in the shower. I pictured myself soaping her back, shampooing her hair, and banging her up against the wall.

I shook my head as I realized I had a woody just even thinking about it. What was I doing? What was she doing? Avery told me Regina had a policy to never shit where she sleeps, and that would, I would assume, include me. After all, Regina was Avery's right-hand woman and I was Avery's brother and roommate. Not to mention, Regina was over at our condo all the time.

I heard the shower running and I had to take my mind off my desire to join her in there, so I rolled a joint and walked over to my balcony. It was a Saturday morning, on Coronado Beach, which meant people were starting to pack the shores. There were people on the boardwalk, rollerskating, walking their dogs and gliding along on scooters and Segways. I took a deep breath, smelling the salt in the air, feeling the moisture on my skin, all while trying to keep my mind out of the gutter. It was no use, though. All I could think about was Regina's naked body and how beautiful it was.

Marijuana helped me think. It had the opposite effect on me than it did for most other people. I was not like my sister, who was typical of the people who smoked weed. She told me that all weed did for her was make her lay on the couch, delay responses to every question, and eat. A lot. She said that when she was high, if somebody asked her a question, she would answer it five minutes later. She didn't like the way that made her feel, so she rarely smoked with me.

But with me, it made everything a bit more clear. Everything burned a little brighter. It was like when you go to an eye doctor and you get glasses for the first time. The doctor would put you in that machine, where they ask you if this picture looks more clear or that one. And, at first, the picture would be extremely blurry. But, after the doctor put his special lens over it, that picture would come into sharp relief. Crisp. That's how it was with me with I smoked pot. Not that my world was blurry when I wasn't smoking weed, but it wasn't as clear as when I did. The clarity of mind was something that really was enhanced with every hit I took on the joint.

That was why I smoked as much as I did. I didn't do it for reasons other people would, to calm down or to feel the high. I did it because it cleared up my head and, at this point, knowing what I did with Regina the night before, my head needed some serious clearing.

I felt my stomach start to turn over and my head was starting to hurt. I was experiencing the first symptoms of a hangover - the first one I've had in a while, because I didn't usually drink to excess. I had gone through my days in college, and in law school, when I would binge drink with the best of them. A fun Friday night was having the guys over with a pony keg of beer, shooting the shit. They would crash on various couches, or on the floor, and the next day, we would have a hair of the dog that bit us.

But I was 26 years old now. I had a job. It was a decent job, with a law firm called Pierce and Wright. They were counting on me to not be a total fuck up. I was determined not to be.

At the moment, Pierce and Wright was giving me assignments where I appeared in court for various people who were involuntarily committed. There are procedures in California that protected them. A person who was a danger to herself and/or others could be involuntarily locked up for 72 hours without a hearing- a 5150 hold. This hold is for evaluation, and, if the person was no longer a danger to himself or others after 72 hours, that person was free to go. If that person was still a danger after 72 hours, they were subject to a 5250 hold and could be held for another 14 days, although they get a hearing, in the hospital, within 4 days. If the person was still a danger after 14 days, they're put into a conservatorship if the person's treating psychiatrist and the psychiatric medical director of the Public Guardian Office sign off on it. Called a 5350 hold, it actually refers to the fact that the conservator makes the decisions about whether or not the person stays in the hospital, not the patient.

One of my firm's specialties was involuntary commitment. I spent most of my time attending various 5150, 5250 and 5350 hearings. Often, the holds were justified, but sometimes, they weren't.

Just then, while Regina was still in the shower, and I was still staring out at the beach below me, my cell phone rang.

"Hey, Aidan, this is Stuart."

Stuart Williams was the managing partner of my firm and was responsible for giving me my various assignments. I was kind of surprised he would call me on a Saturday morning, but, then again, the law never sleeps and neither do our clients.

"Hey Stu, what's up?" I asked him.

"I hate to be bothering you on a Saturday morning. I really do. But one of our clients is in jail right now. Marina Vasiliev. She's been arrested for murdering her husband and she's been asking for you. She wants to hire our firm to represent her in the murder, but she's been very clear that the only person she wants to represent her is you. And she's also been very clear she wants you to come down and see her today. Probably within the next hour or two."

I shook my head, thinking about the splitting headache I had, and the way my stomach was turning somersaults. And I thought about Regina and how I really wanted to hang out with her that day. Not that she wanted to hang out with me. In fact, she probably didn't. But it was worth a shot to ask her.

And if there was one thing I didn't want to be doing on a Saturday morning, it was talking to Marina Vasiliev. She was one of the people I'd represented in 5150 and 5250 hearings. She'd been diagnosed with Borderline Personality Disorder and had been in and out of institutions for most of her adult life.

At the moment, at least before she apparently was arrested for killing her husband, she was back in La Jolla in the enormous house she shared with her husband, Lawrence Murphy. Lawrence was one of those new money guys who made a fortune founding a tech firm in Silicon Valley and leveraging it to found a series of biotech firms right here in San Diego. Biotech was the big industry in the area and was the main reason there was so much money flowing into the city. Everywhere I looked, there were condos going for a minimum of $1.5 million and houses that started at one million.

Lawrence was one of those rich guys. He was the CEO of a firm by the name of Pegasus, which was known not only for being on the cutting edge of discovering new pharmaceuticals, but also being on the cutting edge of human cloning. Animal cloning had been around for quite a while, ever since Dolly the sheep in the late 90s, but, as of yet, there has never been a human cloned. Pegasus was aiming to change that. It was not only involved with therapeutic cloning, which was relatively non-controversial, but was active in animal cloning and were stepping up their game in the race to make the first human clone.

As fascinating as I found Lawrence's job, I did not find Marina quite as fascinating, even though she was gorgeous. She had the kind of pale skin of somebody who never got out in the sun, which was very unusual here in sunny San Diego, and had hair the color of sunset. That was the best way to describe it, other than to say that I had seen her hair color on an Irish setter. It was a deep auburn, with streaks of blonde here and there. Her eyes were Cerulean blue, the color of one of the Blue Topaz rings I bought at a farmers market one day. She was delicate, as brittle as a bird, with slim shoulders, small breasts and a narrow waist. She was the kind of woman who, when she walked in the door, any door, most people turned to get a better look, not because she was odd, although she certainly was that, but because she was gorgeous.

But that didn't really matter. I still didn't want her as a client because she was certifiably off her rocker. She had the manipulative personality of somebody with a deeply rooted personality disorder, which she had. She would literally do anything to get people to do exactly what she wanted. Lying and digging up personal information to hold over people's heads were just a few of the ways she ensured everybody danced to her tune. Sympathy was another one of her calling cards. She would overdose on pills, slit her wrists, cry that somebody was raping her, even though it wasn't true. When all else failed, she resorted to violence. She would attack women and men, clawing their eyes out, kicking, scratching.

In short, Marina was a piece of work.

And, at the moment, she was a piece of work in jail. I

was fully prepared for anything she might say to me and I knew that almost anything she would say would be a flat-out lie. Nevertheless, I would try to get her story. She deserved to be represented by somebody and it sounded like that somebody would be me.

Just then, I turned around and saw Avery coming in the door. She was dressed in her jogging clothes, earbuds in her ears. She had her two dogs, Harlow and Lola, on a leash, and she was out of breath.

"Hey," she said. "What's going on?" she asked as she walked towards her bedroom. I wanted to tell her about what was going on and then I realized I did not want her to know Regina was still here.

"Not much," I said. "I have to see a client today. Which really sucks, because I was hoping I could join the guys later on in the surf." I was talking to Leo and the gang, buds of mine who I usually met with on Saturday mornings. We all made plans to get together about 1 o'clock. It looked like I wouldn't make that particular rendezvous unless I could cut this visit with Marina short, which was what I was hoping for.

I surreptitiously went into the bedroom and saw Regina was out of the shower now. She was dressed in the same clothes as she was last night - black T-shirt, torn and faded jeans, black boots. Her dark hair was up in a pony-tail, and she had on no makeup. She still took my breath away, just as she always did. I was embarrassed to admit that.

What can I say, I'm a dude. Very visual and Regina was definitely pleasing on the eyes.

"About what happened here," I said to Regina. "Maybe we shouldn't tell Avery."

She just shrugged. "She's a grown-ass woman, she can

handle the fact that you and I hooked up last night. No need trying to hide it."

I had to admit, I kind of admired her *I don't give a crap* attitude, but I wasn't all that anxious for Avery to know I hooked up with her best friend and employee.

"Okay, if you insist," I finally said.

"I do insist. Unless you don't want me to let Avery know about us hooking up. And, by the way, this will be the only time. I'm sorry, dude, but sloppy seconds are just not my style."

Her words stung me just a little bit. I wasn't used to a girl treating me like a piece of meat. In fact, I was used to girls who got attached way too quickly. Obviously, that wasn't likely Regina's MO, and I had to admit that I kind of wished it was.

Regina went out into the living room, where Avery was standing next to a small table, sifting through mail. She glanced at Regina, and looked at the mail again, and then glanced up again. And then she cocked her head and smiled.

"I knew it was just a matter of time. What happened, the two of you got schnockered last night and did the deed?" she asked with a smile.

"Something like that," Regina said. "I think I had way too much Grey Goose last night. At least your brother has some taste, in vodka, I mean."

"Whatever, it's your guys' life. Anyhow, Aidan, what were you going to tell me?"

"I have a murder case."

Avery's eyes got wide. "You have a murder case? What do you mean?" She was clearly incredulous. Her mouth was opened and she was just staring at me as if I'd grown another head.

"Why do you say it like that?" I asked her.

"I mean, you've been a lawyer for like two seconds. You just got sworn in last month and your firm's already giving you a case like this?" She shook her head. "Dude, that's a malpractice case waiting to happen."

She was probably right about that. I hadn't been to too many court appearances as a lawyer, aside from a bunch of 5150 and 5250 hearings, which typically lasted not more than a couple of hours. I hadn't yet had a full-blown trial, with multiple witnesses, jury selection and an extensive discovery process.

I shrugged. "What can I say? She's one of my current clients. She was involuntarily committed to the psychiatric unit at Sharp, and she ended up in the Behavioral Health Center in La Mesa. She's been in and out of psychiatric units for most of her life and she landed in the hospital the latest time because she'd threatened to burn down her friend's guesthouse. The friend called the cops and Marina had a meltdown in front of the cops, threatening to kill herself, so she ended up in the psychiatric unit for a 5150 hold. She was deemed to be a danger to herself after the 72 hours, so she was held for another 14 days under a 5250 hold. I represented her in all of these hearings. And now, apparently, she's been accused of murdering her husband."

Avery looked at me. "So, you have a case now that might be capital, and you've been a lawyer for just a few months? What the hell is Pierce and Wright doing to you over there?"

"Sis, I don't know. All I know is that this woman apparently wants me to represent her in her murder case. And apparently she told my firm that it was me or nobody. And I guess she's got deep pockets because her husband was a billionaire. He owned this biotech firm called Pegasus, and —"

"You have the murder case of Lawrence Murphy?" Avery said. "Oh my God."

I took a deep breath. "That doesn't sound good. You immediately knew who I was talking about when I said what she did."

"Who doesn't in this town? Listen, Aidan, when a billionaire gets murdered, especially when the wife is accused of doing it, and especially when said wife has told everybody she knows that she didn't know if she did it because she'd blacked out the night of the murder, that's going to be a story. And here you are, a baby lawyer, hot and heavy in the middle of it. You're going to need some help."

"Well, I guess that's where you come in," I said. "And Regina. My firm doesn't have very good investigators for murder cases. I mean, our firm is a boutique firm, and it doesn't really like to stray from what they do, which is involuntary commitments and class-action lawsuits. I'm going to have to ask my direct supervisor if we can bring Regina on the case. I'm sure that won't be a problem. I'm going to need her help, because you're right, I'll be flying blind with this. The bad thing is, I really don't know why she wants me on her case so badly. I mean, to me, that seems kind of fishy."

"What do you know about this woman?"

"Just that she's borderline. That's her diagnosis. And, considering all the things she's done over her life, I think that's probably the right diagnosis. I mean, I can understand where her personality disorder came from. She was in an orphanage in Russia until she was seven years old. And God knows what happened to her in the orphanage. Her parents were murdered when she was three months old, and she spent all of her time from the age of three months to age seven in an orphanage.

I know a little bit about psychology. Actually, I know quite a bit about it, because that was my major in undergrad. She probably suffered from attachment disorder, which is what happens when a young child is neglected, abused or abandoned. She needed somebody to bond with when she was a baby, someone who could make her feel safe, and she never had that she was very young. I'd imagine she actually experienced horrors in that orphanage. I've read about them, about the kids who are beaten, starved, tied to benches and beds, and some are abandoned. I never really got into her orphanage experiences with her. I'm going to have to definitely talk to her psychiatrist, and her psychotherapist, and everybody who has been working with her to get the entire story about her."

"Okay, so she's borderline. Does she have any lapses of time?"

"I think she does. At least, that's what she tells me. She does tell me, or she has told me, that she would lose entire days sometime. Like it would be Friday afternoon, and the last thing she would remember would be going to the movies the previous Monday. She would have no clue about what happened between those two periods of time. So, yeah. She definitely has had lost time. They call it dissociation."

"So then it's possible that she killed her husband and just doesn't have any memory of it." Avery said. "You're going to have to find out what happened to her."

I looked over at Regina, who was nodding. "Aidan, I'll come with you down to the jail. You want me on this case, right?"

"Of course, you're the best." I clasped my hands in front of me, suddenly feeling shy. This was Regina, a girl I'd known for years. I wasn't used to this. I wasn't used to having my one-night-stand around me after the night had passed. I could smell the scent of her slightly woodsy perfume, could taste the strawberries that were on her lips the night before. I took a deep breath, trying to keep myself from having a boner. That would be embarrassing, to say the very least.

Was my working relationship with Regina going to work? Now that we had broken the seal, so to speak, were we going to be able to just go back to the way we were? This was uncharted territory for me. I wasn't used to seeing my one-nighters again. I was used to women who knew the score, just like I did. Just one night, boom boom boom, and that's it. Yet here I was with my one-nighter going with me to the jail to see his Marina person.

What had I gotten myself into?

"Marina's waiting for us?" Regina asked me.

"She is. Of course, were is she going to go?"

"True that. You driving?" Regina asked me.

"Yeah. I'll buy you lunch."

"You don't have to do that. I got stuff I gotta do in the afternoon."

We said goodbye to Avery, got in my car, and headed towards the jail.

Insanity Defense: Chapter Two

REGINA and I went to the San Diego County jail and waited for Marina to be brought out. I looked over at Regina, who had her hands clasped in front of her, not saying a word. I wondered if she was thinking the same thing I was, which was that last night was a mistake, although it was definitely a mistake I'd like to keep repeating. Not that I could say that to her.

"I was looking at this case, on my phone, on the way over here. What's with this Pegasus thing? They're trying to do human cloning over there?" She shook her head. "I mean, why? That's so weird. Do you remember, God, it was about 20 years ago or more, there was some weird couple on some island who said they'd cloned a human ? And did you ever read that book, *The Boys from Brazil?*"

"No, I can't say I've read that book," I said, impressed that Regina had. I'd heard of that book, but I didn't really know what it was about.

"Well, in this book, these mad scientists cloned Hitler, over and over again, all these new Hitlers, I forget exactly how they were able to do it, because you know Hitler has been dead for so long, but they cloned him. And then they would take these boys, these Hitler clones, and kill their fathers at a certain time, things like that. Because they wanted the baby Hitlers to have the same experiences that Hitler went through. You know the whole nature versus nurture thing. Was Hitler born bad, or was he made that way? Anyhow, these crazy guys wanted these kids to have the same experiences that Hitler did, so they made sure these kids' fathers died at the age of thirteen, or whatever, and they made sure that the father was married to a much younger woman, because those were Hitler's life experiences and the new Hitlers had to have the same experience. I don't remember exactly how it ended. I really don't know what the point is in human cloning. What purpose does it serve?"

"Well, maybe some rich person is going to want to have his daughter cloned because who knows why. I agree with you, however, I do know that cloning has been extremely beneficial in the medical field. You can –"

"I know. People could clone themselves so that they can have excess body parts. You know, you create somebody, exactly like you, and you could store your clone in some laboratory somewhere and just take their liver, or whatever, if you need it. I think I saw a movie like that too, with Scarlett Johansson and Ewan McGregor. I mean, why else would cloning even be a thing?"

"I admit, I don't know. Probably Pegasus just wants to be the first. Just like putting a man on the moon - what was the point in that? I don't really know, but it was important to be the first. Human cloning will be like that."

Regina rolled her eyes. "Yeah, maybe it was pointless to put a man on the moon, but, at the rate we're going, we might have to put people up there to live once we destroy this planet. Besides, the space program has brought a lot of great things to the world, like satellites." She shrugged. "I don't know, but I agree the money going to the moon would probably have been better spent taking care of the people on earth."

Just then, Marina showed up. She was dressed in an orange jumpsuit, of course. Her hair was pulled up in a ponytail and she was wearing no makeup. Still, even though she was extremely pale, she looked like a supermodel. Her blue eyes were clearer than ever, and she walked with the grace of a leopard. Her full lips were pursed as she looked at Regina and me. She was not in handcuffs, either her wrists or her legs, because this was a professional visit, so it wasn't necessary to shackle her.

She sat down at our table, and then looked at Regina and me with suspicion in her eyes.

"Aidan," she said, looking at Regina. "Who is this?" Her eyes bored holes in me. "Aidan, are you cheating on me?"

She smiled as she looked over at Regina and put her hand on Regina's arm. "Soft. You must use good moisturizer. Because I can tell you've been in the sun a lot. You're very tan. You have the kind of skin I've always wanted for myself. Dark."

I was still trying to figure out why she asked if I was cheating on her. I was pretty sure this was meant to be a joke, but, who knows? It was entirely possible she had created a relationship between the two of us in her mind.

Regina just looked at me and shook her head.

Marina looked at me again. "Aidan, are you going to answer my earlier question? Who is this?"

"This is Regina. She's going to be my investigator."

"Investigator. Is that what they're calling it these days?"

She looked at the two of us and smiled. "I can smell it on the two of you. Pheromones. I have a very keen sense of smell. You guys are doing it." She leaned back. "Not that I care. You can do what you want, of course. I just don't know if your lover should be working for you. You're going to get distracted and you're going to do a poor job on my case. That's all I'm thinking."

I didn't try to set her straight. How could I? She somehow picked up on the nonverbal cues between Regina and I, and she had both of our numbers.

"Trust me, Regina is nothing but a professional. And a great private investigator."

"I'll bet," she said.

"And I'm a professional. I won't get distracted by Regina."

"You're a professional?" Marina said with a snort. "You're just a baby. A kid. You're the legal equivalent of Doogie Howser."

"Yet you want me on the case, right?"

"Yes, I do. You see, you're eye candy, Aidan. If I have to go through a nightmare such as a murder trial, when, if you ask me, I should be getting a medal for that man being dead, I might as well go with somebody who's sexy. Like you."

"Marina, that is not the way to pick an attorney," I said, stating the brutally obvious.

"You think I care? Listen, I really don't care whether I live or die. I don't care if I go to prison. I don't care if they put a needle in my arm. I think it would be kind of electric. Just think about all those people on the other side of the glass, watching me die. It gives me shivers of excitement just thinking about it. Also, just think about all those people I can meet behind bars. All the trouble I can stir up.

Quite frankly, I'm very bored with my life as it is. Why do you think I go into the hospital all the time? I live for different experiences, and there's nothing more thrilling than being in a place where people are constantly brought in screaming. Prison is a place where all these damaged lost souls are. All the scared people, all the people who've been tortured throughout their lives. What can I say, I like twisting the knife a little harder. Especially if you're weak. If I go to prison, I'll have my pick of people I can torment."

Regina stepped on my foot, but I was still watching Marina. Regina put her pen down, as she had stopped writing and was just watching Marina with me.

It was then that Maria smiled. "I gotcha, didn't I? You thought that's really what I was after, didn't you? You thought I really wanted to just go to prison so I can torment weak people." She shook her head. "No, that's really not it. I want you to be my attorney, because, quite frankly, I trust you. When you went to my hearing for me, I thought you did a good job. My husband is a billionaire, and believe it or not, I was able to take control of my own personal bank account, don't ask me how I got the money, because you know my husband's assets are frozen at the moment. So I can't get into it. I have my own money, not much, just about $8 million in there. So I can pay you what the firm is asking. One thousand dollars an hour. I just want to have an attorney I like. It's nothing more than that. Besides, six of one, half dozen of the other. Attorneys are all the same. I'm sure you'll do a good job."

Regina resumed her note taking.

I just watched her some more. I didn't know which statement to believe from her - that she wanted to go to prison for sadistic reasons or that she was joking about it.

I decided just to stop trying to figure out the answer to that question, because it was making my head hurt.

"Okay, Marina, I need to ask you some questions about the night your husband died."

She leaned back in her chair. "Go ahead. By the way, you have to get me out of this place. This place stinks like you wouldn't believe, and, quite frankly, this color clashes with my skin and hair. Redheads look horrible in most oranges, especially this particular shade. And the food, don't even get me started. Inedible is not the word."

"I'll do what I can to get you a bond you can make."

"Good," she said. "I have about $5 million to spend on my bond. The rest of my money I have to use to pay for you sharks."

"I'll bring it up at your arraignment," I said. "Now, tell me about the relationship you had with Lawrence."

Marina snorted, which was an odd sound coming from such a small dainty woman. She pursed her lips and I looked away.

"What's there to tell?" she finally said. "I married him for money. Of course. He married me because of the way I look. There wasn't any sex between us, so he wasn't getting much from me. And I certainly wasn't getting anything from him either. But, you know, he helped me to look right at his fancy parties. How not to make a total idiot out of myself in front of people. I needed to go to social functions with him and not drool in front of people and pee on their floor. That's what I did. He had like this entire resumé for me."

"A resumé? What do you mean?"

"A resumé" she repeated. "When he married me, he gave me something that had my name on it and had a job description on there. It was so weird, really. He told me what was expected from me and that he would give me $1 million for every year we were married and no more. So, it kind of was like a job where I earned $1 million a year for not doing a whole lot."

That sounded weird, to say the very least. "I guess I don't really understand. Why would he hire you to be his wife, as opposed to finding somebody who would be his wife for real? The guy was loaded. I'm sure there are quite a few women who are more than willing to marry him."

Marina just shrugged her shoulders. "How am I supposed to know? Besides, the guy was gay. Well, maybe not gay, but definitely bisexual. I don't know the answer to your question, but you have to admit he got off cheap. I'm only getting a million a year, when the guy was worth billions. Any other woman wouldn't put up with that crap. You should be asking me why I got married to him, not the other way around."

"And if he died?"

"If he died, I get nothing more. My prenup says I only get a million a year, and if he died, all of his property goes to charity." She shook her head. "Charity. Not me. Makes me sick, but what can you do? At least you know I didn't kill him to get his money, because I'm not going to get a dime out of his fortune. All I got is the $8 million I've earned over these past 8 years, and I have to pay most of that to you guys. I'll be in the poor house in no time."

That was an interesting twist. It certainly would blunt the inevitable argument that she killed her husband for his money.

"Besides," Marina said. "Even though he was worth billions, most of his money was in Pegasus. I'd rather just take the cash. God knows I wouldn't want to take over for what he was doing there. I think it's unnatural, that human cloning nonsense. Where I come from, you don't do stuff like that."

"So I take it you were not approving of what he was doing?"

"Of course I wasn't. His company is trying to clone somebody just because they can. No other reason. But if they can do it, watch out. We'll have rich guys all over the world creating a clone just so they can have somebody to take over their money when they die, and maybe give them a body part or two along the way. And I read up on the process, with animals. There's always a genetic problem with the second animal, the cloned one. It's always sick. It always dies young. I think the sickest thing in the world."

"You do know that, even though your husband's dead, that cloning project will go on," I asked her. I was starting to suspect that maybe she killed him to stop the cloning project.

"Of course I know that. They got this weird scientist over there heading it up. Dr. Redmond." She shook her head. "You're just trying to nail me on this, any way you can. You're thinking I'm going to confess to killing him to stop him from cloning. I'm telling you I didn't do it. Or at least I don't think I did it."

"About that," I said, "you say you don't think you did it. But you told the cops you have no memories from the night he died. So how do you know if you did it or not?"

She shrugged. "I don't know. I don't remember that day. I don't remember several days before that day."

Grab your copy...
vinci-books.com/insanity-defense

About the Author

Rachel Sinclair was a criminal defense attorney for eleven years, so she doesn't scare easily. She graduated from the University of Missouri-Kansas City School of Law in 1998, and worked for the Public Defender's Office for several years before striking out on her own. She currently lives in San Diego, California, with her boyfriend, Joey, and her two fur babies, Annie and Toby. In her spare time, she likes to read, bicycle all over town, Boogie Board at the beach, and watch trashy television.

www.ingramcontent.com/pod-product-compliance
Lightning Source LLC
Chambersburg PA
CBHW011746010726
47498CB00012B/2950